Petal Pushers

Flower Feud

Petal Pushers

Flower Feud

Catherine R. Daly

SCHOLASTIC INC.

New York   Toronto   London   Auckland

Sydney   Mexico City   New Delhi   Hong Kong

To Ozy and the Biscuit, who make it all possible.

*With gratitude for the wonderfully thorough
copyediting skills of Susan Jeffers Casel.*

*And special thanks to designer Yaffa Jaskoll,
art director Steve Scott, and artist Bella Pilar
for the totally gorgeous book covers!*

❀　　❀　　❀

ISBN 978-0-545-21451-3

12 11 10 9 8 7 6 5 4 3 2 1　　11 12 13 14 15 16/0

Printed in the U.S.A. 40
First edition, March 2011

Book design by Yaffa Jaskoll

Chapter One

"Delphinium Bloom?" called out my homeroom teacher, Ms. Rumble.

I raised my hand, wishing for the millionth time that my parents had given me a more basic first name. Sure, delphiniums are these beautiful, bluish purple flowers. But most kids in my town of Elwood Falls, New Hampshire, don't know that. Which is why I prefer to go by Del.

Ms. Rumble was taking attendance before the morning's announcements. As she went down the list of names, I opened my history folder and looked over my homework assignment on the Civil War. I was glad it was Friday, and I'd have two days off from learning about the Union and the Confederacy.

I glanced up just as Ms. Rumble got to Sammy Washington. He's a bit of a smart aleck, so he answered with a "Yo," which earned him a frown from Ms. Rumble. But then we were done, and just in time.

The loudspeaker came on, and the assistant principal's voice rang out. Yada yada yada. Yearbooks would be on sale in the cafeteria starting next week. Final exams would begin June 18. And lockers would need to be cleared out by June 21.

I only half listened. I had already preordered a yearbook, and the dates for locker clean out and finals were marked on my calendar. And yes, in case you were wondering, I *do* know that my organized ways may seem a bit excessive. My family doesn't call me "Detail Del" for nothing. I choose to take it as a compliment. (Do I really have a choice?)

But then the principal said something that made me sit up with, not with interest, but with another feeling — dread.

"And now," he said, "we have a special announcement from seventh-grade student council representative, Ashley Edwards."

Ashley Edwards is my number one enemy. And she's the worst kind of all — the one you *used* to be best friends with. Okay, that was all the way back in preschool, so any info she might have to use against me is of the "she spilled grape juice all over her Barney T-shirt when she was three and a half and cried for an hour" variety, but you get the picture. These days she is super mean and the two of us barely speak, except when she's making fun of me.

I stared up at the loudspeaker with a frown and nervously ran my hand through my wavy, shoulder-length, light brown hair. Whatever Ashley had to say, it couldn't be good. The rest of my classmates seemed interested, however. A hush had fallen over the classroom. Ashley is pretty and wears trendy clothes and people seem to like her. Or pretend to like her because she's popular. I'm never quite sure how these things work.

Ashley's annoyingly chipper voice came through loud and clear.

"Fellow students of Sarah Josepha Hale Middle School, I have some very exciting news to share with each and every one of you," she began. I rolled my eyes. What a drama queen! "As you all probably know, it is prom season — the most exciting and fun time for high schoolers. Well, why should *they* have all the fun? So I had a fab idea — a *middle school* prom!"

Middle school prom! I thought. *What* an awful *idea*. I

looked around at my fellow students. Surely they realized how silly this was . . .

"OMG!" cried Alice Ambrose, who sat a couple of seats ahead of me. "What a great idea!"

Everyone else started grinning and nodding. I rolled my eyes. What were my classmates *thinking*? They had all been to our last school dance — a Valentine's Day event called Have a Heart. Boys on one side of the gym, girls on the other. Ice-cold pizzas congealing in their boxes and bottles of flat soda. To add insult to injury, the music had been provided via iPod by one of the teachers who was obsessed with the Beach Boys. It was a middle school dance, not a fiftieth reunion! My best friend, Becky, and I were so bored we called our parents to pick us up early. Seriously underwhelming.

But apparently everyone except me was suffering from a case of Bad Middle School Dance Amnesia.

Ashley continued. "The theme is A Night in the Tropics, so the gym will be decorated to look like a gorgeous tropical island. And yes, I know what you're wondering," she added with a laugh. "You *are* going to need a date! So ask out your crush from gym class or that cutie from science lab. Buy a gorgeous gown, rent the coolest tux, and show up at seven o'clock on Saturday, June ninth for the best dance that Sarah Josepha Hale Middle School has ever seen!" She paused, then added, "If I do say so myself!"

I could feel myself fuming. I knew "Your crush from gym class" was a direct reference to Hamilton Baldwin, the new boy in school.

Some people meet cute. Hamilton and I met totally awkward, one day in the hallway as I was picking spinach out of my teeth. Hamilton is tall, with longish, sandy-colored hair, and these deep blue eyes. And he's really sweet and funny. We're friends. (My boy-crazy friend Heather may say otherwise, but that's all it is.) Still, knowing that Ashley Edwards was angling to take Hamilton to the Moronic Middle School Prom made me mad. Just a little.

"Thank you, Ashley," said the assistant principal. "And I'd like to add that tickets will be on sale from any student council representative."

The loudspeaker shut off with a crackle and everyone started talking excitedly, about what they were going to wear and who they might ask.

I saw Rachel Lebowitz turn around in her seat so quickly her long straight brown hair nearly whipped Mike

Michaels in the face. (That's his name, I'm not making it up.) She was grinning. "How cool is that!" she cried. "A middle school prom! Can you believe it?"

I shook my head. Rachel was one of Ashley's hand-maidens. *Of course* she thought the prom was the greatest thing since strawberry lip gloss.

It was just like Ashley to rush things. Why wait till high school to have a prom like everyone else? This was the girl who got her first French manicure when she was in preschool. So it made sense. But why was everyone else falling for it?

Then the bell rang for second period and I gathered up my books and headed to history class. I didn't give the dance another thought until lunchtime.

The cafeteria was serving chicken fingers, which always puts me in a good mood. Especially if they don't run out of honey-mustard sauce before I get there. Not taking any chances, I didn't even drop off my books, and went straight to the cafeteria line. I noticed that I was three people behind Hamilton, who was wearing a denim workshirt with a small hole on the shoulder. He balanced two orders of chicken fingers on his tray. The boy has a huge appetite.

I grabbed three containers of sauce, just to be safe, then placed my food on top of my books. I carefully approached the table where I sit every day with my four closest friends. Jessica Wu, spacey and funny (sometimes on purpose, sometimes not), was dressed in a ruffly shirt and leggings, her short, black hair spiking up adorably. Amy Arthur, with her reddish brown hair and rectangular, black glasses, was wearing jeans with deep cuffs and a pink-and-red striped T-shirt. Amy can keep a secret like nobody's business. Heather Hanson, with her dimples and corkscrew dirty-blonde curls, looks like a princess in a storybook. But she's tougher than she appears. And last but not least, there was Becky Davis, my very best friend. Tall and slim, Becky looks like a model but doesn't know it. She has jet-black shoulder-length curls, big brown eyes, and flawless, dark brown skin.

Becky gave me a distracted wave as she flipped through one of her notebooks.

"Hey, guys," I said. I put my tray down and settled myself onto a stool.

"Can you believe it?" squealed Heather.

"Believe what?" I asked, intrigued. I glanced at my friends.

I hadn't seen Amy look so happy since the day her sister and her cheerleader friends had taken her to see the last Harry Potter movie and hadn't made Amy sit all by herself in the first row, like they usually did.

"The middle school prom, of course!" Amy said.

"Oh, that," I sighed. I hadn't thought my friends would get sucked into the madness, too.

"Yes, that," said Heather. "You mean, you're not totally excited about it?" She looked shocked.

I picked up a chicken finger and dunked it.

"Not really," I said, taking a bite. Mmm — crispy deliciousness.

"I don't think Ms. Studious over here is excited, either," said Jessica, pointing a thumb over at Becky. My BFF was studying her notes intently as she ate her favorite lunch — her mom's homemade chicken salad on whole wheat with the crusts cut off.

Becky glanced up and smiled at me. "Hey, Del," she said. "Rumor is Ms. Herbert might give a pop quiz this afternoon."

I nodded sympathetically and swallowed. I was glad someone besides me wasn't taken in by this stupid prom idea of Ashley's.

"You guys!" Amy sputtered. She looked from me to Becky, exasperated. "Do you have any idea how awesome this is? Amber has been talking about nothing but the prom for weeks. So I already know *everything* — where to go to get the best dresses, the coolest shoes, the prettiest jewelry." She looked around at us. "She's a varsity cheerleader you know. Co-captain."

We all hid our smiles. Amy is very proud of her popular big sister and mentions this thrilling piece of information every chance she gets.

I shook my head. "How is this dance going to be any different than all the others?" I asked. "Except of course that we'll be all dressed up while we're bored to tears?"

"What do you mean?" asked Jessica.

"Anyone remember Have a Heart?" I asked pointedly.

Jessica made a face. "That *was* lame," she said.

Heather shook her head. "I think this one might be different," she said. "Ashley may be mean, but I bet she knows how to throw a great party."

I shrugged. "Won't we have time for fancy proms when we're in high school?"

A look of disappointment crossed Heather's face. Then suddenly she grinned and turned to Amy. "Can you ask Amber where to get the best prom . . . *flowers*?" she asked, looking right at me as she said the last word.

Amy cocked her head. "Sure!" she said. She thought for a moment. "Funny, she's talked about everything *but* prom flowers. I wonder why."

"Flowers?" I said, perking right up.

Heather laughed. "I knew that would get your attention."

My family owns a flower shop. It used to be the only flower shop in town (more on that later) and was called Flowers on Fairfield (more to come on *that*, too). My grandparents used to run the store and it had always been my refuge from my messy, disorganized house. But then Gran and Gramps decided to move to Florida and leave the store in my parents' hands. It's been a tricky transition, but we're trying to make it work.

So the fact that we now had a middle school prom in addition to a regular prom to sell flowers for *was* an exciting prospect.

"Maybe I spoke too quickly," I said, barely able to suppress my grin. "A Night in the Tropics actually sounds pretty amazing to me. Bring on the corsages!"

I thought about all the extra business the store would get. I was glad tomorrow was Saturday, when I worked all day at the store. Mom and Dad were going to be psyched to hear the news.

"So I can count on you all to get your prom flowers from us, right?" I asked my friends.

"Of course!" said Jessica.

Amy suddenly looked nervous. "But what if . . . nobody asks us? Can we still go?"

Heather shook her curls. "That's impossible!" she said. "We'll have dates. All of us." She bit her lip. "I think."

"I don't see why we can't just go stag," I said. "That means alone," I explained, anticipating Jessica's question.

"I don't know," said Jessica. "Ashley *did* say you need dates." She frowned. "Do you think one of us should ask Ashley if it's okay to go . . . stag?"

"Don't look at me," I said. "I'm certainly not asking her. I'm not even sure I'm going to this stupid prom."

Becky finally glanced up from her notebook, looking confused. "Did you say *prom*?" she asked. "What's going on?"

"Oh, Becky!" cried Heather and Amy in unison.

I patted my friend on the hand. Only Becky could get so caught up in studying she totally missed what was apparently the most exciting news of the school year.

No wonder we're best friends!

Chapter Two

The next morning, I woke up fairly bursting to tell my family the news about the middle school prom. The night before, Mom and Dad had been in a huge rush to leave the house to go out on a long-postponed date night, so I hadn't had time to fill them in.

I had been left in charge of my three younger sisters, Rose, Aster, and Poppy. (My parents say they save money on hiring babysitters because I'm so responsible. This makes me happy, though I'd be happy to accept payment at any time. . . .) The four of us played board games — Chutes and Ladders for Poppy's sake, and then Cranium, for us older girls. It had taken a while to find all the pieces to the games, which were thrust haphazardly into the top of the hall closet. I'm talking Clue pieces in the Mouse Trap box and Battleship pegs in Pictionary. My parents are the most disorganized people I know.

I thought I'd make my announcement over breakfast. But Mom had to leave for the store early to let in a painter. After cramming the last bite of an everything bagel with chive cream cheese into my mouth, I headed out after her. Dad, Rose, Aster, and Poppy were all running late and would follow. My big news would have to wait until we were all together in the store.

While Mom got the store in order, she let me do one of my favorite tasks: start a flower arrangement. I stood at the worktable, sniffing a pink sweet pea as I contemplated exactly where to place it. The arrangement was being sent to my old fourth-grade teacher, Mrs. Stanley, who had just had her appendix out, so I wanted it to be especially pretty and cheerful. I had just positioned the sweet pea next to an iris when the phone rang. I glanced up. Mom was nowhere to be seen. I walked to the front counter and answered.

"Flowers on . . ." I started to say, then caught myself. "Oh, sorry, I mean Petal Pushers!"

"What time are you open until tonight?" the caller wanted to know.

"Six thirty," I told her. I replaced the receiver and

sighed. It had only been a week since we had changed the store name, so it was no wonder I couldn't get it straight.

Mom appeared, a broom in her hand. She was wearing a pretty, printed kerchief over her wavy, light brown hair and a cute striped dress. She started sweeping up.

"Nope," I said, wagging my finger at her. "Remember? Rose and Aster will be here soon. We'll let *them* sweep the store."

Mom smiled. "That's right," she said. "Today is their first official How-to-Work-in-a-Flower-Shop lesson."

I nodded. My twin ten-year-old sisters had been all excited about working in the store, but, of course, they only wanted to do the fun stuff. Rose loved greeting the customers and Aster liked making arrangements of dead flowers (it's a goth thing; don't ask). It caused some serious friction between us. I mean, I had helped out Gran and Gramps in the store for years before *I* was allowed to do that kind of stuff. Mom and Dad had decided that my sisters could help out, but that I was allowed to teach them the ins and outs of the flower business.

Mom leaned the broom against the wall. "Fine with me," she said with a grin. Cleaning isn't really her thing (to say the least), so she was glad to pass it on. She gazed out the front window, which had been cleared of flowers and was now filled with a rather large man in coveralls who was scraping off the old store name.

And by old, I mean ancient. FLOWERS ON FAIRFIELD had been SERVING YOUR FLORAL NEEDS SINCE 1912. The painter, who was at that moment working on the *s* in Flowers, would soon be painting our new name "Petal Pushers" in bright and cheerful colors.

The new name is cute, huh? Poppy came up with it. She's only five and she's full of surprises.

Mom sighed. "It's a little sad to watch the old name disappear, isn't it?"

I, too, felt a twinge of sadness. I worried that we were making too many changes all at once. But I decided to channel Becky, who always looks on the bright side of every-thing. "It's progress!" I declared. "You're changing things up with your new arrangements. Things are being updated."

Mom smiled at me gratefully. "I guess you're right." Still, she looked melancholy.

The bell above the door rang as my twin sisters walked inside. Dad and Poppy had stopped at the play-ground before heading to The Corner Café to pick up coffee for Dad and a muffin for Poppy — their Saturday morning ritual.

Aster looked around the store, taking everything in quietly as is her habit. Rose, on the other hand, shrugged out of her cropped denim jacket and deposited it on the counter. "Gorgeous!" she squealed, looking at my half-finished bouquet. She took a bright pink rose from the arrangement, clipped it with the shears, and placed it behind her ear. I was annoyed that she had disturbed my arrangement, but I decided to let it slide. The flower *did* look pretty against her gleaming blonde hair. It also matched her bubblegum pink T-shirt perfectly. Rose is super-girly and dramatic. She's an aspiring actress and gets the lead in almost every school play.

Aster, her twin, was clad in black tights, black boots, and a black dress under a moth-eaten mustard yellow cardigan that I think used to belong to Gramps. I couldn't help but smile at my sisters, who were complete opposites, yet somehow shared a room and got along just great. Go figure.

I left the "Get Well Soon" arrangement for Mom to finish, knowing she would add something interesting to it. People had really been remarking about the change in the flowers since Mom and Dad took over. Don't get me wrong,

Gran and Gramps did beautiful arrangements. But Mom had lots of fun, creative ideas with stuff that you wouldn't imagine putting into a bouquet. For instance, she had placed a pale blue plastic dinosaur from the toy store in the middle of the "Baby Boy" arrangement she'd sent out yesterday. The new mom had called to tell us how cool and different it was.

I took a deep breath and faced my sisters. I knew this was going to be difficult. It always is when you're sharing something special that once belonged just to you.

"Welcome to Flowers . . ." there I went again! "Petal Pushers," I corrected myself. "Today we're going to learn Flower Shop 101." I picked up a folder off the counter and took out a sheet of paper I'd worked on that week.

I saw Rose and Aster glance at each other and roll their eyes.

"Step one," I started, ignoring them. "Opening up. This includes sweeping, wiping down counters, and cleaning out the cooler and the buckets."

I handed Rose a rag and some spray and she began wiping down the front counter. I pointed Aster in the direction of the broom and she went right to work, making a tidy pile of leaves and dust.

"Step two," I went on. "Checking voice mail. New orders may have come in since closing the day before. If there are any emergencies, you deal with them immediately."

"A flower emergency!" said Rose, pausing and holding the rag over her heart. "Like when the mayor was allergic to the flowers in all the centerpieces and we had to remove them the night before the wedding?"

"That's right," I said. "Or once, when Gran and Gramps were still here, an arrangement was accidentally delivered to the wrong address. The guy who got it was so excited to get flowers that he refused to give them back. So we had to make a whole new one really fast. You never know what will come up."

"When do we start designing arrangements?" Rose asked.

I sighed. "We have more work to do. One of you can clean the bottom of the cooler of any leaves, petals, and stems, and the other can clean the buckets out."

"I'll take the buckets," said Rose quickly. She gets cold easily and wanted to spend as little time in the cooler as necessary.

Ten minutes later Rose was kneeling over a bucket and

giving me a very dirty look. "You didn't tell me this would involve a *toilet brush*," she said. I laughed. It's the easiest way to clean the flower buckets, along with a squirt of soap and some bleach. But it's not one of my favorite tasks, either.

When the cooler was cleaned and the buckets were scrubbed, Rose and Aster looked at me eagerly.

"Step three," I said. "The fun part! Our supply of premade bouquets is pretty low. We need to arrange them."

Aster and Rose cheered. "What are premade bouquets?" asked Rose.

"For people who are in a rush," I replied. "Who don't have the time or the money for an arrangement to be made especially for them."

Rose smiled. "A man rushing to meet his long-lost love at the bus station," she said dreamily.

"A mourner on their way to the cemetery," said Aster.

"Someone running late to a birthday party," I said, bringing them both down to earth.

Rose made a face at me. "Bo-ring."

Aster laughed.

We made an assembly line and ended up with these

bright, springtime bouquets of purples and yellows, and cute round yellow flowers called billy balls for an accent. Mom nodded her approval as she put the finishing touches on Mrs. Stanley's arrangement. "Nice work, girls!" she called. Rose and Aster both grinned.

Aster wrapped the bouquets in colorful tissue paper and cellophane, and Rose was on ribbon duty. We made short work of the task. I blinked. Maybe having some help around here wasn't such a bad idea after all.

"Look at my girls working together!" cried Dad. We looked up. We hadn't even heard him come in the back door. Poppy, her favorite velvet evening bag looped over her shoulder, sat high up on his shoulders, eating a very large muffin and getting crumbs in Dad's hair. She waved merrily from her perch.

Dad deposited my littlest sister on the far end of the counter, where she finished her muffin, happily kicking her feet. Dad kissed Mom hello and rested his elbows on the counter, Saturday's paper fanned out in front of him. Poppy fished her new doll, Blanche, out of her evening bag and started grabbing leftover floral, tissue, and ribbon odds and ends to make a tiny bouquet for her.

"Blanche is getting married today," she said out loud, to no one in particular.

I was going to say something about how unprofessional it was to have Poppy sitting on the counter, but I held my tongue. I had more important things to focus on. Finally, everyone was there, together, and I could share my news!

I cleared my throat. "Guess what?" I began, and my family swiveled around to face me. "My school is having a prom. It's called A Night in the Tropics."

"Sounds like fun, Del!" said Mom.

"OMG, what?" Rose shrieked. "You're going to get your *very* own prom? You're so lucky!" She reminded me of Heather and Amy.

Aster rolled her eyes. I was glad *one* Bloom sister was being sensible.

"Um, not really," I replied. "I mean, Ashley is in charge of the whole thing, so you can imagine how annoying it's going to be. But," I added, glancing around at my family, "*Petal Pushers* is lucky. Because now we'll get twice as much business!"

"That's true!" Mom said, beaming at me. "We'll have

kids from the high school *and* the middle school coming in for corsages and boutonnieres."

Dad let out a low whistle. "That's great!"

"I know," I said. "How many prom orders have we gotten so far?"

Mom wrinkled her nose. "Two or three, I think," she said.

Two or three? "Are you sure, Mom?" I asked. "The prom's in a couple of weeks. That doesn't sound right at all."

Mom shrugged. "I'm sure all the kids are procrastinating," she said.

Hmm. Mom is the number one procrastinator in the world, so of course she'd choose that as the reason.

"Well, I can work on the middle schoolers at least," I said. "Some of them might not even know they should buy prom flowers. I'll remind them where the best place in town is."

"Thanks, hon," said Mom.

"What's a prom, anyway?" Poppy wanted to know.

"Only the coolest thing ever," answered Rose. "They're held your junior and senior years of high school. You get to buy a gorgeous dress. A boy asks you to go. He buys you a corsage to wear on your wrist, and you buy him a boutonniere."

"That's a flower to wear on the lapel of his suit," I explained to Poppy.

Rose continued. "Sometimes there's a theme. Like Under the Sea, or A Night on Broadway." She smiled. "That's what I hope mine is."

Mom and Dad glanced at Rose, clearly amused by her enthusiasm for an event that she wouldn't be attending for at least six years. Unless the middle school prom tradition continued . . . which meant Rose would get her wish in a mere two years.

Ugh.

"I don't understand," I said to Rose. "How do you know so much about proms?"

"Totally obsessed," explained Aster. She knows her twin better than anyone.

Rose wasn't finished yet. "You get your hair done. You should get a manicure and pedicure. You get beautiful shoes to match your dress. And some places, the prom is in a fancy hotel." Her eyes were shining, as if this was the most wonderful thing she could think of. Besides getting a standing ovation at curtain call, of course. "There's a band or a DJ and they play all this great music and you dance the night away with your friends and you slow dance with your date. It's a beautiful, romantic night," she concluded.

Mom and Dad looked like they were trying hard not to laugh.

"So how were *your* proms?" I asked them. "Beautiful and romantic?"

Mom grew up right here in Elwood Falls. Dad is originally from Long Island in New York. They met at a party when Dad was in grad school in Boston, and Mom was visiting a friend. Dad was standing in the corner when he saw Mom by the refreshment table. He walked over, picked up a piece of fruit and asked, "'Do I dare to eat a peach?'" And luckily, my mom did not run screaming. Instead, she turned to him and said, "'I shall wear white flannel trousers, and walk upon the beach.'" Well, that was it for Dad. She was beautiful *and* she could quote from "The Love Song of J. Alfred Prufrock," a poem by T. S. Eliot. They fell in love and a year and a half later they were married.

"I actually never went to my prom," Mom replied. "I bought

this totally cool vintage dress and I borrowed some amazing rhinestone jewelry from Gran. And Gramps made me an extra-special corsage as a surprise, which my date was supposed to bring over. So I was sitting in the living room waiting for my date to come get me. Finally, his mom called — he got food poisoning from some bad clams and couldn't go."

"Ew," said Rose, making a face.

"Why didn't you just go on your own?" I asked.

Rose looked aghast at the very idea.

Mom shrugged. "None of my friends were going stag and I didn't want to be the only one," she said. "What a waste of a beautiful dress. And I never got to see my special corsage, either."

Rose was frowning. Then she brightened and turned to Dad. "How about you?"

I was fairly certain she was barking up the wrong tree. And I was right. Dad shrugged. "Who had time for proms? I had a big project due the next week. I spent the whole weekend in the library doing research!"

"Oh, Dad," Rose groaned. "Really!"

"It was for extra credit!" he protested. "I graduated high school with a four point four!"

Rose looked totally disappointed. "One night, Dad. The most magical night ever."

Ring-a-ling-ling! The bell over the door rang as a customer pushed it open. I wiped my hands on my apron and turned to Rose and Aster, forgetting the prom issue for a moment. "Our first customer of the day!" I whispered. "When a customer comes in, you should greet them almost immediately. Make them feel welcome, but don't pressure them. Rose, would you like to do the honors?"

Rose smiled. This was her favorite thing to do. But before she could speak —

"So it's true!" said a thin, familiar voice belonging to an elderly lady. "What in the world is going on here?"

This was no customer. It was our Great-aunt Lily. And she didn't look very happy at all. She was angrily pointing at the painter standing in the window, who was now looking a little nervous.

Aunt Lily has that effect on people. Me especially.

"Aunt Lily!" said Mom, heading over to give her mother's sister a kiss on her papery cheek. "How lovely to see you."

Aunt Lily snorted. "Are you telling me that there has been yet another change made to the store that I own one

27

third of?" she said in her icy, clipped tone. "One third, Daisy! And no one had the decency to tell me?"

Eek. I gave Mom and Dad a baleful look. Aunt Lily did have a point. I knew I should have reminded them to tell her about the name change. They're so forgetful sometimes.

"I'm sorry," Mom said. "We should have called you right away. We discussed it with my parents and . . ."

"And to find out about it the way I did! At the Ladies Auxiliary Luncheon! By none other than Gladys Hockenpfeffer." Aunt Lily made an irritated face. "She's such a busybody. I was completely taken aback!"

I gulped. I had to step in and try to fix things. "Actually, Aunt Lily, the new name was inspired by you."

Aunt Lily turned around. "Delphinium," she said with a curt nod.

"Remember those clothes you lent Rose for the play she was in? We all liked the cute little pants — the pedal pushers — and when Poppy called them *petal* pushers, we realized that would make a great new name."

For a second it looked like Aunt Lily might actually smile. But she regained her composure and shrugged.

"Fine," she said. "What can I do with you all? Anyway, we have a much bigger issue than the store name."

My stomach jumped. Oh no. What could it be now?

"May I ask how many prom orders you've gotten so far?" Aunt Lily asked.

"We were just discussing that," said my mom. "Not so many. But Del just told us there's going to be a middle school prom, too, so we're feeling optimistic . . ."

Aunt Lily cut her off. "As I suspected," she said. "It seems as if our rival is trying to take away our business. Again."

"What do you mean?" I asked. My heart sank. I knew this couldn't be good.

"Benjamin, would you please hold up the paper?" commanded Aunt Lily.

Dad complied, lifting the paper so we had a full view of the front and back pages. And what we saw made us gasp.

The entire back page of Saturday's paper was an ad. An ad for Fleur. There was a photo of a girl's wrist with a simple orchid corsage on it. Under the photo were the words:

FLEUR.

ELEGANT. SOPHISTICATED. STYLISH.

WHY GO ANYWHERE ELSE FOR YOUR PROM FLOWERS?

Fleur is our competition. The new, fancy florist in town with software so you can design virtual bouquets. Fleur is in the mall, is twice as big as Petal Pushers, and has tons of flowers we didn't normally carry.

And there's one more part of the Fleur story. The store is owned by Hamilton Baldwin's mom. Yes, Hamilton Baldwin — the new guy in school who I think is cute. The guy in gym class who Ashley has a crush on. But Hamilton doesn't know I know his mother owns Fleur.

As if things weren't complicated enough.

Mom took a closer look at the ad. "Oh my," she said in a small voice. "It says 'Become a Fleur Fan on Facebook'!"

So Fleur was at it again. Last month they had tried to steal away our first big job — a large wedding. Luckily, we had managed to keep it. Now they were taking out newspaper ads and creating Facebook pages. I glanced around our store. It was sweet, small, and very old-fashioned. We had no website, no virtual bouquets, and certainly no Facebook page.

"So you think everyone is going to Fleur instead of

us?" Dad asked with a frown, putting down the paper.

"Yes," said Aunt Lily. "Especially if they're doing a lot of advertising."

Mom cleared her throat. "I'm sure all the kids will start coming in this weekend."

"I am, too," said Dad optimistically. "I'll bet we have a line out the door this very afternoon!"

"I hope you're right," Aunt Lily said. But she didn't look convinced. I didn't feel convinced, either. "Good day," she said. She gave us a curt nod and marched out the door.

We all stared at each other after she left.

"Well, I think that proms sound bee-you-tee-ful," Poppy pronounced. "Mommy, can you make me a corsage?"

"Another time, my love," said Mom. "I have to start another arrangement. Del, can you help me?"

I busied myself cutting flowers for the new arrangement. But inside I was fuming. I couldn't believe Fleur was trying to take away our prom business.

This means war! I thought.

Chapter Three

After dinner that night, I was more determined than ever to beat Fleur at their own game. Despite Mom's and Dad's optimism, we hadn't had a single prom customer that day.

While Rose and Aster went to their room to read, and Mom put Poppy to bed, I headed straight to my room — and the computer. I had never been on Facebook before, but I figured it had to be pretty easy since so many people, including my friends' parents, spent so much time on it.

I typed FACEBOOK into the search engine, and the page popped up. Did I want a personal page? No. I clicked CREATE A PAGE. This was easy. LOCAL BUSINESS. What did I want to name my page? Why, PETAL PUSHERS of course!

Next, I had to review the terms of use. So much to read! It all seemed fairly straightforward until one thing jumped off the page at me: YOU WILL NOT USE FACEBOOK IF YOU ARE UNDER 13.

Of course. I should have known that. None of my friends are on Facebook yet. I thought about Hamilton. Was he thirteen already? He could have been. I didn't know when his birthday was. Maybe he'd even been the one to suggest creating a Facebook page for Fleur! I gritted my teeth at the thought.

I asked my parents to come to my room. Mom was in her pale yellow chenille bathrobe, rubbing almond moisturizing cream into her hands like she does every night. It smelled good. Dad was in a T-shirt and the goofy pajama bottoms with big red hearts my sisters and I had chipped in to give him this past Valentine's Day.

"What's up, sweetie?" asked Dad, yawning.

"I want to set up a Facebook account for Petal Pushers," I explained.

"That's a good idea," said Dad. "If Fleur can do it, why can't we?"

"My thoughts exactly!" I replied. "But I need someone thirteen or older to log in."

"Well, I am definitely older than thirteen," Mom said with a smile.

I punched in her e-mail address and we came up with a password. After we filled in all the info, I stared at the blank page. I felt seriously overwhelmed and wasn't sure where to start.

"Maybe I'll look up Fleur's page to see what they did," I said.

"Hey," said Mom suddenly. "Could you look up Elizabeth Hennessey?"

"Who?" I asked.

"She was my best friend in elementary school," explained Mom. "I've always wondered what happened to her."

"Really, Mom?" I said. "Right now?"

"Why not?" she said eagerly. "I've never been on Facebook before."

I typed in the name and several Elizabeth Hennesseys popped up. Mom squinted at the screen, trying to determine if one of them was her long-lost friend. "Here, let me sit," she said, all but pushing me out of the seat.

Mom clicked on a couple of pictures before she found one that looked familiar. "I think this is her," she said. "But I can't see all her info. Should I . . . 'friend' her?" She looked at Dad.

"Why not?" he said.

"Oh, this is very exciting!" she said with a giggle.

Dad leaned over her shoulder, a smile on his face. "Let's look up Manny Elgarresta," he suggested.

"Enough, you guys," I said. "We have work to do!"

"It will just take a minute," said Dad. "Manny and I started the Dungeons and Dragons club at my high school," he said. "I don't want to brag, but I was a Level Twelve Dwarf Fighter!"

Mom and I gave each other alarmed looks. Just when I think I know every nerdy fact about my dad, he goes and surprises me.

Then Dad got that look on his face he always gets when he is about to quote literature. He's an English Lit professor, so it goes with the territory. "'The companions of our child-hood always possess a certain power over our minds which hardly any later friend can obtain,'" he said. "Mary Shelley."

"Hmmm, I wonder if Matt Whelan is on here," Mom considered aloud.

Dad smirked at Mom. "Wasn't he your boyfriend in ninth grade?" he asked. Mom bristled.

Enough was enough. "Let's look up Fleur's page," I told Mom.

I changed places with her and checked it out. Fleur had a link to their website and pictures of some okay-looking arrangements. Then I laughed.

"Well, now we know they're not stealing away customers with their Facebook page," I said.

"How can you tell?" Mom asked curiously.

"Look at the number of fans," I said, tapping the screen. "Three. And two of them have the last name Baldwin."

I did notice that none of the Baldwins was Hamilton, which made me feel somewhat better.

It was clear that Facebook was not the answer we were looking for. I told my parents good night and gave them each a kiss, and they left me to my planning. But I was too tired to think much more, so I went to sleep.

I wasn't in the best mood as I trudged to school on Monday morning. But it was a sunny day, so it was hard to stay sour. The birds were singing, the flowers were blooming, all that good stuff. I took a deep sniff — relishing that springy smell of fresh dirt and newly mown grass. Then I stepped over a bunch of extra-large earthworms writhing on the sidewalk. Yuck. I wondered if Dad would be able to get Poppy to school in time — she is fascinated by the creepy-crawly things and would want to stop and study each one.

When I got to school, I made my way to the cafeteria. I liked to avoid the mad morning locker rush and hang out with my friends over a hot chocolate or orange juice.

I spotted Becky, Heather, Amy, and Jessica at the table already. I wondered if Amy would have a funny story about Amber, or if Becky had some gossip from her mom, who works at the local paper. I'd be happy to talk about anything, just as long as it wasn't the middle school prom. I had been thinking about it, one way or another, all weekend.

"You have to help us decide," Heather said breathlessly as soon as I sat down. "Prom dates — do we wait for someone to ask us, or do we ask someone ourselves?"

I fought back a groan. I looked at Becky, but my BFF was buried in one of her notebooks again. We had had a long conversation about the prom insanity that weekend. She *had* said that she wanted to go, just to check things out. And we had heard that Ashley had confirmed that you could go stag if you wanted to. So I'd reluctantly agreed to go, too.

"Amber's friends are doing both," said Amy. "But Amber, of course, was asked out by the captain of the football team." She looked around at us. "She's the head cheerleader — it's like a rule or something."

"If you could go with anyone, who would it be?" Jessica asked Amy.

Amy was silent for a while, but finally confessed that she thought Brian Kilpatrick was cute. "He's got blond hair and blue eyes and he's really funny," she said. "I think he'd be the perfect date. What about you, Heather?" she asked.

Heather lowered her voice and leaned forward con-spiratorially. "I've been thinking about this all weekend. I've decided I want to go with Billy Walters," she said. "I hope he asks me."

Billy Walters? He may have been the captain of the soccer team now, but I would always remember him as the boy who, in third grade, asked the school librarian where to find books on World War Three. She had been completely aghast.

"Heather, I had no idea you were so old-fashioned," I joked. "That's very traditional of you. You could ask him yourself, you know."

Heather looked embarrassed. "I know. But I just can't."

Becky finally looked up from her notebook and we smiled at each other. Thank goodness for Becky. She was my port in the storm of girly girls gone boy crazy.

Jessica, in a surprisingly practical way, announced that she was going to ask Jackson Bates. Their moms had gone to college together so Jessica and Jackson had been friends since they were in diapers. "I don't *like* him like him," she said. "And he doesn't *like* me like me. But we'll have so much fun!"

"So what about you, Becky?" asked Amy. "Are you crushing on anyone?"

I snorted. "No way!" I said. "Becky doesn't have time for crushes! And neither do I."

"Wait a minute," said Heather, scrunching up her face in disbelief. The table went silent. Then I realized that everyone was looking at me.

"What?" I said, feeling uncomfortable.

"Well, what about Hamilton?" Heather asked.

My cheeks reddened. *Hamilton.* He'd been on my mind all weekend, too — but not in an asking-him-to-the-dance way.

"There's something I have to tell you guys," I said, my

voice low. I hadn't yet told Jessica, Amy, and Heather about the Hamilton–Fleur connection. (I had already shared the news with Becky, of course.)

They all leaned in, their eyes wide.

I took a deep breath and blew it out before I spoke. "You're never going to believe this," I said. "Hamilton's mom is the owner of Fleur."

Three pairs of shocked eyes looked back at me.

"You mean the new flower store in the mall?" Amy gasped.

"Well, it's no wonder he knew that a delphinium was a flower!" said Heather.

I nodded.

"Does he know your family owns Flowers on Fairfield?" Jessica asked.

"Petal Pushers," Becky and I corrected her at the same time, then grinned at each other.

"Whatever," Jessica said impatiently. "Does he?"

"I don't think so," I said slowly. "I certainly didn't tell him."

"I don't see why it's such a big deal," said Heather. "Ask him!"

I looked at her in shock. "Even if I wanted to, I can't," I

said. "He's the competition. Did you see the ad Fleur took out in Saturday's paper? They might as well have said 'Don't go to Petal Pushers, we're so much cooler.'" I shook my head. "I'm not even sure I should be friends with him anymore."

Everyone stared at me worriedly.

"Hey, who died?" asked a snotty-sounding girl behind us. We all spun around.

Ashley Edwards stood there, her long, blonde hair gleaming, her plaid, drop-waist dress adorable and wrinkle-free. She looked, as usual, like she had stepped right off a runway and had somehow ended up in a New Hampshire middle school.

"Why the long faces?" she went on. "Aren't you all totally psyched for my middle school prom?" She turned to her two best friends who stood slightly behind her like bodyguards. "It'll be just like a real prom, only better. Totally brill if I do say so myself."

"Right," Sabrina and Rachel said in unison. I blinked at them. They were so interchangeable it wasn't even funny.

Ashley put her hands on her hips. "So are any of you asking anyone in particular?"

"As if we'd tell you," said Heather, tossing her corkscrew curls.

Ashley leaned in over my shoulder. "How about you, Del, hmmmm?"

"None of your business," I said.

"Look, girls," she said to her friends. "Del is being mysterious." She narrowed her eyes and stared at me for a moment, then laughed. "Ta-ta, see you around."

Amy turned to me, all serious. "You should get over this Hamilton problem," she whispered. "Otherwise Ashley's going to ask him to the dance."

"Fine with me," I said between gritted teeth. "Becky and I will go stag together, won't we, Becky?"

Becky glanced at me, looking slightly bewildered. "Um . . . sure," she said.

"But what if Hamilton tries to ask you, Del?" Heather pressed on. "Are you going to turn him down?"

I crossed my arms and squared my shoulders. "Hamilton is not going to ask me because he's not interested. End of story."

Heather sighed.

"But just in case your crazy idea happens to be right," I added defiantly, "he won't be able to ask me. I'll just avoid him. I don't want to talk to him, anyway. It won't be hard."

Famous last words.

Chapter Four

The next day, I was minding my own business, standing in the lunch line when someone tapped me on the shoulder. I turned around warily.

"Hey, Del!" Hamilton said cheerfully. "What's up? Haven't seen you in a while." He grinned. "What, have you been avoiding me?" he said jokingly.

I gulped. Hamilton pushed his shaggy hair out of his eyes. He has the longest eyelashes I had ever seen on anyone, boy or girl.

I wasn't quite sure how I felt — a weird mix of happy to see him, angry at him about the Fleur ad, nervous that he would ask me to the dance, and maybe, oddly enough, nervous that he wouldn't.

"Hi, Hamilton," I replied. Then, not knowing what to do, I picked up a package of chocolate chip cookies and studied the nutritional content like it was the most interesting thing I had ever seen.

Hamilton laughed. "Fascinating, huh? I prefer reading oatmeal raisin myself." He picked up a package and pretended to study it as well. I couldn't help it, I laughed. He was just so goofy. And cute. Goofily cute. Totally distracted, I realized that I was next in line. I grabbed a sandwich and a drink and paid the cashier without even registering what I was doing.

"Bye, Hamilton," I said. He waved.

When I got back to my seat I looked down and saw I had grabbed a grape juice by mistake. I hate grape juice. Too sweet and purply.

My friends were poring over prom magazines that Amy had borrowed from her sister. My face was still hot from my brief encounter with Hamilton and I couldn't pay attention. I nodded enthusiastically when Heather asked me what I thought of a certain dress, then wanted to take it back when I realized I had given the thumbs-up to a bright pink fringed flapper-style dress. Becky gave me a funny look.

"Well, what do you think about *this* one?" Amy asked the group, pointing to a white dress that had so many silver sequins on the bodice that it looked like an ice skater's costume.

No one knew what to say. Finally, Heather broke the silence. "Totally tacky," she said bluntly.

"And the bubblegum-pink flapper dress wasn't?" Amy asked, her feelings clearly hurt.

"Del liked it!" protested Heather.

Amy turned to me. "Do you really like the flapper dress better than the sequined one?" she asked me point-blank.

"Hey," I said, hurriedly grabbing my books. "Gotta go. It's the perfect time to start reminding people to buy their prom flowers at Petal Pushers!"

My last class of the day was science lab. I ran into Albert Bustios, my lab partner, on the way there.

"I'm really excited about today's lab," he said.

"I know! Acids and bases!" I replied.

Yes, I like science lab. A lot. I like how organized you need to be to perform the experiments. And when everything is just right, you get the exact result you're looking for.

"Totally. I mean, they're only the key to understanding

chemistry!" he said with a smile. "I heard Ms. Studdert is going to use cabbage juice as the neutral."

"Nice choice," I said.

"I have an idea!" said Albert excitedly. "Let's take turns testing the solutions and keep them secret from each other so we can guess which is which."

"That's a great idea," I said. "It will definitely make the lab more interesting." I smiled at him. That was why Albert was the best lab partner ever. He just got it.

We walked into the lab room together. Our teacher, Ms. Studdert, is one of my favorites. She's young and pretty and makes science fun. There's just one thing I don't like about science class: Bob the Bully. Make that *two* things I don't like: Bob and his obnoxious lab partner and best friend, Matt. The two of them are disruptive and annoying. You'd think that Bob's broken leg would slow him down a bit. But maybe his cast was itching him or something, because that day he was being even more annoying than ever. If that's even possible.

Ms. Studdert, wearing a crisply starched white lab coat, stood in front of the room. She clasped her hands together, hardly able to contain her enthusiasm.

"Today we're going to do one of my favorite seventh-grade science experiments ever — acids and bases!" she said with a grin.

Albert and I smiled at each other. The rest of the class looked bored. Bob gasped loudly like he was crazy excited. "How thrilling!" he cried.

Matt laughed.

Ms. Studdert gave Bob a warning look, and held up a red cabbage, neatly cut in half. "We're going to make cabbage water today and then we're going to . . ."

"Have a party!" cried Bob.

Albert and I exchanged disgusted glances. Leave it to Bob to try to ruin the best experiment of the school year. I turned around and glared at him. He stuck out his tongue at me. So immature. I faced the front of the room and shook my head. Bob would still be irritating if he were at least funny. But his jokes are always so lame.

"Robert," said Ms. Studdert in a warning tone. Her normally kind face had a harsh expression on it. "Please keep your comments to yourself."

"Sure, Ms. St-St-Studdert!" he replied.

Matt snorted with laughter.

I spun around in my seat, my mouth open in shock. The room began to buzz. Had Bob really just made fun of a *teacher*? This was shocking, even for Bob. I'm no expert, but that screamed instant detention to me.

Apparently, Ms. Studdert was taken aback, too. She stared at him in disbelief.

"Robert, that's it," she said sternly. "You will report to detention immediately after school today."

Yes! I thought, smiling to myself. Bob would finally learn his lesson.

"Oh man," Bob groaned, and Matt said, "Tough break, dude."

"And that's not all," Ms. Studdert went on, "you and Matt together are a bad combination. New partners for you both. Right now."

Oh no! Albert and I exchanged nervous glances. We both dropped our eyes to our notebooks, willing ourselves invisible. Because when teachers split up the bad students, you know who they reassign them to. The good ones. It was like we had targets on our backs.

There was silence, during which I assume Ms. Studdert was scanning the room, deciding who to torture. I was concentrating on my blank notebook page with all my power. *Say someone else's name,* I chanted silently. *Please.*

"Albert," she finally said. "You will be Matt's new partner. Matt, please go join Albert."

My eyes flew to Albert's face. He looked as stricken as I felt.

I knew what was coming next, but I still hoped against hope that somehow I was mistaken.

"Del, you'll have to move to the back of the room to join Bob, if you don't mind."

I do mind! I wanted to scream, but I knew I couldn't.

Albert gave me a doleful look. Matt approached our table and I gathered my books. As I started to walk past Matt, I paused to glare at him.

He shrugged. "Sorry, Del," he said.

"Your apology is not accepted," I told him.

I made my way to the back of the room and plopped down on the lab stool next to Bob.

"Hello, Delfurnit —"

I raised my finger to his face to silence him. I was not in the mood. "Listen to me, Bob," I snapped. "I take science seriously. If you mess up this experiment I'll . . ."

"You'll what?" he said with a smirk.

"I'll . . ." Hmm. He was right in a way; he already had detention. What could I do that was much worse? Break his other leg? Too violent. Tell his mom? Too second grade. Send him a bouquet of dead flowers from the store? Too Aster. Finally, I got it. "I'll make you do this lab all by yourself," I threatened. That would fix him.

But it didn't.

Things started out okay. Ms. Studdert handed out safety goggles and materials. I placed several pieces of cabbage into a large beaker and covered them with hot water. But as soon as the water cooled down, my new lab partner picked up the beaker, drank the liquid, and burped. My mouth fell open in shock. This was beyond gross, even for Bob. I had to start all over again, making a second batch of cabbage juice and telling Bob not to dream of drinking it. Then I lined up my solutions — ammonia, baking soda, lemon juice, vinegar, cream of tartar, and seltzer. I stole a glance at the clock. We were running out of time thanks to Bob and his shenanigans. That was a Gran word, and it totally fit.

I took a medicine dropper and added some lemon juice to the cabbage water. Then I added a few drops of vinegar to the next one. I watched excitedly, waiting for them both to change color.

But something was not right. "These are both acids," I said, more to myself than to my ridiculous lab partner. "So why is one turning green and the other red?"

Bob snickered. "Because I mixed them all up, Delfrozenyogurt!" he cried.

I stared at him in disbelief. Everyone else was finishing up and dumping their compounds down the sink. When the bell rang I really did want to break Bob's other leg. Or at least dump an acid — and maybe a base — on his head.

I took a couple of deep breaths to calm myself before I packed up my backpack and made my way to the front of the room. "Ms. Studdert," I said, "can I stay after to redo the experiment? Bob messed the whole thing up."

Ms. Studdert sighed. "I'm sorry, Del. Of course you can." She shut her eyes for a moment. "I just don't know what to do with him. He's smart, but he's such a smart aleck." She patted my arm. "I'm sure you'll end up setting a good example for him."

Albert stopped by on the way out the door. "I missed

you today, Del," he said. But then he smiled. "But Matt wasn't so bad, actually. We had fun."

I scowled at him. "Lucky you," I said.

After dinner that night, Mom and I sat at the kitchen table finishing up dessert. It was Rose and Aster's turn to clear. Dad was helping out, scrubbing the pots and pans, his sleeves rolled up.

"Any prom orders today?" I asked hopefully, taking a spoonful of chocolate pudding.

Mom looked glum. "Not a one," she said. She lowered her voice. "I don't want to panic, but where are all our customers?" she asked worriedly.

I shook my head. "I've been reminding all the kids at school to go to our store," I said. "Could they really be going to Fleur instead?" I put down my spoon and carried the bowl to the sink. I had lost my appetite.

The phone rang, and Dad reached out a soapy hand to answer it.

"Bloom residence," he said. "Yes, just a minute." He held the receiver to his chest. "Rose, it's for you."

Rose looked pleased. "Hello?" she said. "Oh, *hello*."

She gave us all an excited look and took the phone into the living room.

Curious, I lingered in the kitchen.

A couple of minutes later, Rose replaced the phone, checked to make sure it was really hung up, and started shrieking.

"Guess what?" she said.

"What?" I asked.

"I got invited to Jennifer Collins's slumber party!" she exclaimed.

"Um . . . sounds great," I said.

"How nice," said Mom, wrapping both her hands around her cup of tea.

"Nice?" said Rose. "Nice? It's . . . it's . . . stupendous!"

"Nice word," Dad said appreciatively.

Aster dumped a handful of forks into the dishwasher and yawned.

"What's so stupendous about it, sweetie?" Dad wanted to know.

"Well, she's just the most popular girl in the entire fifth grade," Rose explained. "Tell them, Aster," she urged.

"She's popular," Aster agreed with a shrug.

Rose's eyes were shining. "She has this party every year. And this year she invited me! They order pizzas. Watch movies. Do makeovers. Give each other manicures. It's — amazing!"

"Sounds incredible," I said drily. *As incredible as my middle school prom!*

Aster snickered.

"Are you going, too, honey?" Dad asked Aster.

"Nope," said Aster, emptying a water glass and placing it in the top rack of the dishwasher.

Rose bit her lip and looked at Aster worriedly. Dad handed Rose a frying pan to dry. "Do we know Jennifer's parents?" he asked her.

Mom looked up. "Yes. Maybe I should give them a call . . ." she started to say.

"Mom!" Rose squealed. "That would be humiliating! Oh my God, you can't possibly do that. Do you understand how embarrassing that would be? I would be the laughingstock of the entire fifth grade!"

I wasn't in the mood for any more of Rose's drama that evening, so I grabbed our dog's leash. Buster, our adorable black-and-white Boston terrier, had been lingering around the garbage can hoping someone would drop some scraps. I snapped the leash on his collar and pulled him out the door. He gave me an annoyed look.

Buster was rather unadorably sniffing at my neighbor's garbage can when my cell phone rang. I flipped it open. It was Heather. "Hey, Heath —" I started to say.

"I've got it!" she announced. "You and Hamilton and this flower business thing. It's a star-crossed romance — like Romeo and Juliet."

I rolled my eyes. "We're reading that play in my English class, too," I said. I wasn't going to indulge Heather in her silly fantasies.

"Don't you see?" she pressed on. "Your families are at odds so you cannot be together." She sighed. "It's so romantic."

"It's so ridiculous," I responded. "Come on, Heather, don't you think you're taking things too far?"

Heather grew silent. "I know you like him," she said. "And I bet you anything he likes you back. Who cares if his mom owns a flower shop?"

Just hearing the words *Hamilton*, *mom*, and *flower shop* made me see red. *Why did they have to move here and ruin everything?* I thought. I yanked Buster's leash, perhaps a little too forcefully, and we set off down the street. "You just don't understand, Heather," I said. "Petal Pushers means everything to me. And it is really important to keep the store running for my grandparents." I gulped, thinking about Gran and Gramps, millions of miles away. Knowing them, they were on some sunset cruise somewhere, and didn't warrant any pity. But I wanted to make them proud. And being friends with the enemy just did not make sense.

"I'll tell you what I *do* understand," she said. "That you are going to be really upset if he goes to the dance with Ashley."

I felt a jab to my heart. *I must have eaten too much chili at dinner,* I told myself. "He can go with whomever he wants," I said. "It's just not going to be me."

"Whatever you say, Del," Heather answered. She changed the subject, slightly. "Hey, did you hear that Carmine Belloni finally got up the nerve to ask Penelope Peterson to the prom? And she said yes!"

"That's great," I said, meaning it. Carmine was a really good guy. He'd been crushing on Penelope for months. I was glad *someone* was happy.

Chapter Five

Later that night, I lay in bed, stewing. The Blooms couldn't just sit back and let Fleur take over as *the* flower shop in town. I had to find out if all the kids were really going to Fleur instead of us to order their prom flowers — and why. Was a newspaper ad really enough to steal all our business?

Finally, I couldn't take it anymore and walked over to my bookshelf. I searched until I found an old dog-eared copy of *The Wolves of Willoughby Chase*, an old favorite. The adventures of wild Bonnie and her delicate cousin Sylvia as they tried to outwit their evil governess, Miss Slighcarp, would be just the thing to take my mind off proms. I had just settled under the covers when there was a knock on my door. I sighed and put the book facedown on my quilt.

"Come in," I called. Rose slipped in, looking furtive.

She was wearing her pink robe with the hearts on it and fluffy white slippers. She sat down on my bed. She looked so pensive I almost started to laugh. But Rose can get insulted easily, so I kept a straight face.

"I'm worried about Aster," she whispered.

"Why? Is there a sudden shortage of black nail polish?" I couldn't resist asking.

Rose gave me the fish eye. "Del-phinium," she said, drawing my name out. "Did you see the serious look on her face when I got the call from Jennifer?"

"Was it any more serious than usual?" I asked.

"She was sad, Del," Rose explained. "She's upset that she wasn't invited to Jennifer Collins's birthday party and I was." She sighed. "What am I going to do?"

I wrinkled my brow at Rose. Was she kidding?

"So you're telling me that goth girl Aster is jealous that you are going to a girly sleepover that she's not invited to?" I shook my head. "I think you're wrong. Totally wrong. Aster doesn't do parties. Remember? For your guys' birthday she wanted to visit Edgar Allan Poe's grave in Baltimore."

Rose put her hand on my arm. "Del, she's my twin. I understand these things."

There was no arguing with Rose when she was convinced of something, no matter what the evidence was to the contrary. "Whatever you say," I told her. "But I wouldn't worry too much. I think she'll survive."

But Rose had that determined look on her face she sometimes gets. "I can fix this," she said, her jaw set. "I have to."

"Good luck," I said. She nodded seriously, stood up, and walked to the door. "Good night, Del," she said, her hand resting on the doorknob. "Don't worry. I have a plan." She closed the door behind her with a click.

I picked up my book with a sigh. If only *I* had a plan. I finished the first chapter, replaced my bookmark, checked to make sure my alarm was set, and turned out the light.

"Hello, Delphotobooth."

Blech. "Hello, Bob," I said with a sigh, not wanting to turn away from my locker. I hung my jacket up extra slow, savoring the moments before I had to face him. "And to what do I owe the pleasure of your company?" I asked sarcastically.

"Huh?" said Bob.

"Skip it," I said, turning around. "So where's your little sidekick, Matt?" I asked. "I didn't think you two did anything without each other."

"I don't know where he is, actually," said Bob with a frown. "Listen, Del, I need to copy your lab sheet," he said. "It's due today."

"Um, yeah," I said. "That's why I redid the entire thing after school yesterday."

He stared at me.

"The lab that *you* ruined," I reminded him.

"Yeah, and now I need it," he said. "So hand it over."

I laughed. "No way," I said.

"But I'm going to fail!" he whined.

"Too bad," I said. "You should have thought of that before you messed up our experiment." I slammed my locker shut.

"Del, you're being a real pain," he said.

"It takes one to know one," I replied. I wasn't proud of myself for the elementary school retort. But it fit. I took off down the hall.

Ashley, Rachel, and Sabrina were standing by Ashley's locker and had witnessed the whole thing. "Ooh, did you get into a fight with your *boyfriend*?" Ashley called out as I passed by.

Her handmaidens cackled merrily. I felt my face turn bright red. Without even thinking, I stopped right in front of her. "What did you say?" I asked in a low, angry voice.

"JK!" she said.

"Huh?" I asked.

"Just kidding," she explained slowly, like I was a little kid. "Text much? Don't be so touchy, Delphinium. It's unattractive."

And then she and her handmaidens laughed and took off down the hallway.

Ugh. What a great start to my day. I arrived at our cafeteria table to find Becky there, alone. For once, she wasn't buried in a notebook, but just sitting with her hands folded in her lap, her brown eyes sparkling.

"Hi, Del," she said, a big smile on her face. She took a deep breath. "I wanted to . . ."

I sat down heavily and slammed my books on the table. "Bob is the biggest idiot I've ever met!" I told her. "Can you believe he asked to copy my lab sheet after he messed up the experiment and I had to redo everything by myself?"

"That's terrible," said Becky. "I hope you said no."

"Of course I did!" I sputtered. "The nerve! It's all because he and his stupid friend Matt got Ms. Studdert so mad she made them change partners. It's not fair — those two deserve each *other*."

Becky frowned. "Bob certainly is a big idiot." She paused. "But is Matt really that bad?"

"Anyone who's friends with someone like Bob *has* to be an idiot, too," I said. "Right?"

"Right," said Becky in a small voice.

"Now what did you want to tell me?" I asked her.

Becky opened her mouth, then shut it. "Oh, nothing important," she said.

"Hey, guys!" said Heather cheerfully as she sat down at the table, her cheeks flushed. "Guess what?"

"You asked Billy Walters to the dance," I guessed.

"No," said Heather with a huge grin. "He asked *me*!"

"Oh, wow!" I exclaimed. I realized that I felt a little jealous that Heather was going to the dance with someone she liked. I decided to rise above it. "So what do you like about him?" I asked her eagerly.

Heather leaned forward, her lips pressed together as if

she was holding back a big secret. "Well, he's very cute and very popular," she confided. "He's the captain of the soccer team, you know. Everyone likes him."

I gave Heather a funny look. Becky seemed as confused as I felt. "But what do *you* like about him?" she asked. "I mean, is he funny?"

Heather looked blank.

"Do you like the same kind of movies, maybe?" I suggested.

"Or you're both really into . . . history?" suggested Becky.

Heather glanced at us as if we were crazy. "He's *popular*," she said. "All the girls want to go to the prom with him. And he asked — me." She smiled smugly.

"Oh," I said. Becky gave me a barely perceptible shrug. That was why we were best friends. We understood each other without even speaking.

Heather looked a little disappointed that Becky and I were not completely ecstatic about her big news. But Amy and Jessica soon arrived and their reaction more than made up for it. General squealing and mass excitement.

"This is the best news I've heard all week!" said Jessica.

I squinted at her. "Jessica, it's only Wednesday morning."

She brushed me off. "You know what I mean."

Amy had news herself. "Well, you know how I was hoping that Brian Kilpatrick would ask me?"

"So he did?" asked Heather excitedly.

"No," Amy admitted. "But Angela Cash told Ellen Corker that Jimmy Matthews is planning on asking me. Maybe even today."

"That's great!" I said.

Amy held up a hand. There was more to come. "So I'm wondering if I should ask Brian before Jimmy asks me."

I was confused. "But don't you like Jimmy?" I asked. "He's so funny. I bet you'd have a good time with him." I took a deep breath and said what was on my mind. "Why not just go with him instead of waiting for an invitation that might not ever come?"

"Oh, I would have a good time with him," Amy agreed. "But he's just not as cool as Brian."

I still thought she was wrong. But I leaned forward,

interested despite myself. "Have you ever asked a boy out before?"

"Never," Amy said, her eyes wide behind her glasses. "It makes me feel sick to my stomach just thinking about it, actually."

I could imagine. Not that I had ever asked a boy out myself. And not that I ever would, at the rate things were going.

That evening Mom was making her famous turkey and sun-dried tomato meat loaf, and the house smelled delicious. I hoped she wouldn't burn it. (It's happened more than once.)

I washed my hands and galloped down the steps to the kitchen. I was hungry.

Everyone was already sitting at the dinner table. Mom stood by the oven, waiting for the timer to go off.

"Any orders today?" I asked her. I asked this every night now, and the answer was always the same.

Mom frowned. "No," she said slowly. Then she pasted a big smile on her face. "I have a new attitude," she said. "The power of positive thinking. I guarantee that the store will be flooded with orders this weekend." She nodded. "Plus, I called Gran today. She's going to say a prayer to Saint Jude."

"You told Gran?" I wailed. "Now she and Gramps are going to worry!"

"The patron saint of lost causes?" called Dad from across the room.

I laughed. Mom's family is Irish Catholic and Dad's is Jewish and they are both fascinated with each other's religion. Dad insists we get the biggest Christmas tree in the lot every year and he knows all the saints and their sometimes strange specialties. And Mom spins a mean dreidel and her brisket is out of this world. They crack me up, those two.

"That's him," said Mom with a grin. She turned to me. "Gran and Gramps still own two-thirds of the business," she said. "It seemed irresponsible not to tell them what was going on." She paused. "Also, better they hear it from me . . ."

"Than Aunt Lily," I finished. "All right, you've got me there."

I headed over to the old wooden kitchen table where my sisters sat, practically salivating as they waited for dinner to be served. Rose had a huge grin on her face and looked like, as Gramps would say, the cat that ate the canary. And I was pretty sure it wasn't because we were having meat loaf for dinner.

I was right. "Aster," Rose prodded. "Tell everyone what happened today!"

Aster scrunched up her face, pretending to think hard. "Um, Aiden threw up in gym class?"

"Ugh," said Mom with a grimace. The timer went off and she grabbed two oven mitts, which Poppy likes to call "helping hands," and took the meat loaf out of the oven. "Really, Aster, not at the dinner table," she added, setting the meat loaf on a trivet in the middle of the table.

"Don't touch," I warned Poppy, who was reaching out for the food. "It's superhot."

"Not that, silly," Rose said to Aster. "Your big news."

Aster looked like she wanted to say something sarcastic, then thought better of it. "Yes," she said with a small smile. "I was invited to Jennifer's slumber party."

Rose clapped her hands together prettily. "Isn't that just so exciting?" she cried.

"I guess so," said Aster, concentrating on building the perfect orange mountain of mashed sweet potatoes.

"Well, that's very nice news," said Dad, coming in and sitting down at the table. "I'm glad you girls are going together." He frowned as he concentrated on slicing the meat loaf.

"Nice," repeated Aster. Then she looked up. "I'm just not sure why she asked me," she said.

"Obviously, she likes you!" Rose answered quickly. "Why else would she ask you?"

"I don't know, Rose," said Aster, looking at her twin pointedly.

"She likes you, silly," Rose repeated. "She wants to be your friend."

Later that night there was another knock at my door, and Rose walked in, biting her lip.

"Can I tell you something?" she asked.

"Sure," I said, putting down my Spanish textbook. I had a test tomorrow and was doing some last-minute studying. I would probably dream in Spanish. Don't laugh, it's happened before.

"I am the best sister ever!" Rose exclaimed. "No offense."

"None taken," I replied.

Rose cleared her throat. "I asked Jennifer to invite Aster to the party. Did you see how happy she was?"

"Um, yeah," I said. Happy? Was Rose losing it? I gave her

a look. "Are you *sure* Aster's really and truly excited?" I asked.

"Of course she is!" exclaimed Rose. "She just got invited to the coolest party of the whole year. She's the envy of every girl who isn't going. Why wouldn't she be excited?"

I stared at Rose. "I just want to make sure that it's really *Aster* who's happy about it."

Rose gave me a quizzical look.

"And not just you," I explained.

"It's definitely Aster." She nodded her head. "Definitely Aster."

"Whatever you say, Rose. You know best."

Rose nodded and stood up. "Just don't tell Aster I arranged it. Or she'll never want to go."

"Okay," I said, picking up my textbook.

"Thanks, Del," she said before leaving the room.

My cell phone, sitting on my bedside table, beeped. I had a text message. I picked it up eagerly. But it was only a homework question from Jessica. I was surprised to discover I felt a little disappointed. After all the prom excitement at school, I had been expecting something juicier.

69

Chapter Six

"I have good news and bad news," Mom said the next night as we were loading the dishwasher after dinner. "The good news is that Del's work has paid off. We've finally gotten some middle-school orders."

"Whew," I said. "But what's the bad news?"

"The bad news is that both of our high school orders were *canceled*." Mom said.

"Canceled?" I cried, my spirits sinking.

"Yes," said Mom grimly. She bit her lip. "Do you think this means all the high school kids are going to Fleur?"

"It has to," I said. "There's nowhere else to go."

"I wish I knew some high school kids," Mom said, her shoulders sagging. "We could ask them what's going on. Why they prefer Fleur. Why we're being replaced."

I had an idea. "I'll text my friend Amy," I said. "Her big sister is a junior at the high school. She'll know what's going on."

Mom looked relieved. "Good idea, Del," she said. "Maybe if we know what we're up against, we can do something."

CAN U ASK YR SIS Y EVRY1 IS GNG 2 FLEUR 4 PROM FLWRS? I texted later. I pressed SEND. And waited.

In a couple hours, my phone rang. "Sorry it's taking me so long to get back to you," Amy said. "But Amber's still not home yet. She's at a pep rally. Cheerleading, you know."

"I know," I said.

"So if I don't get to ask her tonight, it will have to wait till tomorrow. That okay?"

"Fine," I said with a sigh. "It's not like we can do anything about it tonight, anyway." I held the phone against my ear with my shoulder and worriedly peeled a strip of pink nail polish off my thumbnail. Now I'd have to take all of it off. What a mess. "So what's the latest on the Jimmy/Brian front?" I asked.

"Well, Jimmy asked me," she said with a sigh. "But I said no. I just have this feeling that Brian will come through."

I grimaced. "That must have been awkward."

"Kind of," she admitted.

"A bird in the hand is worth two in the bush," I said. It came out of my mouth before I even realized what I was saying. *How very Dad of me,* I thought.

"Huh?" asked Amy.

"It's from *Aesop's Fables*. Kind of like an invitation from a guy you think is nice is worth more than a possible invite from someone else. You know?"

"I guess so," she said slowly. "But I already said no. And Jimmy already asked Eleni Nikolopolous instead. And she already said yes."

Eleni was in my math class. "She's really nice," I said.

"I know," Amy said glumly.

None of this was making very much sense to me. Heather wanted to go with someone for the sole reason that he was popular. Amy had turned down a real invite from a nice, funny guy (who was also cute) for a phantom date.

Amy and I said good-bye and she promised to text me if she had news.

I pressed END and sighed. This prom date business was getting out of control. I needed to talk to someone who understood. I pressed number one on my speed dial — Becky. It rang once and went straight to voice mail. I knitted my brow. Had Becky just ignored my call?

I hung up without leaving a message.

I woke up the next morning to a text from Amy. GOT THE 411! it said. MEET ME IN CAF THIS AM.

I got to school bright and early. I was the first one at our table in the cafeteria. I sat down and waited. And waited.

Amy finally showed up, her cheeks flushed. "Sorry, Del. I was hanging out by my locker for a little bit thinking Brian might pass by, but he never did."

I shook my head with a grin. You had to hand it to her — she wasn't giving up so easily. "It's fine," I said. I leaned forward eagerly. "So what's going on?"

Amy placed her palms on the table. "I have good news and bad news. Which do you want first?"

Couldn't I ever just get some plain old good news? I considered it. "The good news," I said. Might as well postpone hearing the bad for a moment or two.

"The good news is that Amber and her friends are not going to Fleur for their prom flowers."

"Really?" I cried, my mood instantly brightening. "That's great! So everyone must be procras —"

"Here's the bad news. They're not going *anywhere* for their flowers. Amber says that corsages are just not cool," Amy explained. "And if Amber says they are not cool, nobody thinks they're cool. That's the way it works when you're cohead cheerleader."

"Oh," I said. It felt like someone had punched me in my stomach. How could *flowers* not be cool? They were the most amazing, beautiful things ever. I just didn't get it.

"I'm sorry, Del," said Amy, breaking the silence.

"Thanks, Amy," I said, remembering to be polite. But I kind of wanted to put my head down on the table and cry.

I spent the rest of the day with a heavy heart. I had asked Becky why she hadn't returned my call the night before, and she gave me some lame excuse, so I was feeling weird about that. I dreaded telling my family the news from Amy. I also dreaded going to gym class. I had successfully avoided Hamilton all week. But there would be no escaping him in gym class. Plus, my new lab partner, Bob, would be there, too. He was unable to participate thanks to his crutches, but totally able to make fun of everyone from the sidelines. What a way to end the week!

I changed into my gym clothes morosely. My mood certainly did not match the garish purple-and-yellow outfit I was wearing. Dad had fallen behind on his laundry duties again, so I had no gym socks and was forced to wear the not-meant-to-be-seen knee socks I'd had on under my jeans — and they were red-and-white striped. I shouldn't have, but I looked at myself in the mirror before I headed out the door. I totally looked like a clown.

When I walked into the gym, Ashley took one look at me and shrieked, "Where are my sunglasses? Del is blinding me!"

I barely even glanced her way. I had more important things on my mind.

"Hey," Ashley went on in a loud whisper. "How are things with Bob?"

I gave her a quizzical look. I wasn't sure, but I thought I could feel Hamilton's eyes on my back. I didn't turn around to confirm.

"You know, your *partner*," she said meaningfully.

I opened my mouth to reply. But then, said partner spoke up and added insult to injury. "Did you get dressed in the dark, Del Frito-Lay?" he shouted.

Tweet! Our gym teacher, Mr. Rolando, blew his whistle and we all looked his way. "I thought we'd take a break from basketball today," he said. Some kids cheered and others groaned. I decided to withhold my reaction until I heard what the alternative was.

"So instead I have a treat — an oldie but a goodie. Today we are going to play Steal the Bacon!" he said cheerfully.

This time *everyone* groaned. Myself included.

"A fine, friendly game that tests your speed and agility," he boomed. He smiled. "I used to love to play Steal the Bacon in gym class back at Saint Nicholas of Tolentine School," he said. He divided us into teams and gave us each a number from one to twelve. Then he placed a gym towel on the floor. "This is the bacon," he said solemnly.

He explained that he would randomly call a number and the two kids with the same number would walk up to the towel and circle it. Then one kid would grab the "bacon" and try to run back "home." If that kid made it back, that team got a point. If they got tagged, the other team got the point. It was simple, he said.

And awful, I thought.

The only game I could think of that was worse than this was musical chairs. Not too long ago, that game had been a staple at almost every birthday party. I can still remember making it to the bitter end, circling the remaining chair, warily eyeing the boy or girl who, until that moment, had been a friend and was now a mortal enemy. Then the dive for the chair. And one person triumphantly sitting, the other unceremoniously ending up on the floor.

"Number four," called Mr. Rolando. I watched as two kids ran up to the towel and begin circling it.

"Grab it, grab it!" called Bob from the sidelines. "Do something!"

Finally, Rob Chambers grabbed the "bacon" and ran back "home" as fast as he could. Maria Gonzales didn't stand a chance. *My team is losing at Steal the Bacon,* I thought. *And my family is losing business that they really need. What are we going to tell Gran and Gramps?*

"Number ten," called Mr. Rolando.

I watched as Fred Jacobs, a kid from the other team, approached the towel — I mean bacon. Then I watched as he grabbed it and ran away. *Uh-oh,* I thought. *Some dummy forgot their number.*

"Del, what are you doing?" one of my teammates yelled.

Oh no. That dummy was me! I stood up but it was too late. Fred was jumping up and down, having scored a point for his team. I hadn't even tried to stop him. How humiliating.

"Way to go, Del!" shouted Bob sarcastically. Ashley, who was on the other team, saluted me. I couldn't even look at Hamilton, who was also on the other team.

Mortified, I stared at the floor. I hated Steal the Bacon. I hated Bob. I hated Ashley. And I definitely hated the prom, too. It was totally distracting me.

At the end of the class, I trudged out of the gym, my eyes on the scuffed floor.

"Hey, Del!" said a voice. I groaned. It was Hamilton. I had almost made it.

"Hey, Hamilton," I said weakly.

"I hate Steal the Bacon," he said with a grin. "We used to play it all the time at my old school. One time I stole it and this kid tackled me and almost pulled down my gym shorts."

I laughed despite myself. He may have been the enemy, but he was still very funny.

"So I wanted to ask you a question," he said.

My heart flew to my throat. Oh no! What if he was going to ask me to the dance? I quickly changed the subject.

"You know what's worse than Steal the Bacon?" I asked. "Nothing! Well, maybe square dancing. Remember square dancing?" I rattled on. We had just completed our square dancing unit, so the chances that he didn't remember it, quite vividly, were slim. "That was not much fun, was it? Boy, I really didn't enjoy that class. Basketball, I don't mind. But Steal the Bacon and square dancing are the two worst. For sure."

Hamilton was looking at me bemusedly. By this point we were at the girls' locker room door. "See you!" I said as

I yanked the door open and scooted inside. As the door swung shut, I caught a glimpse of his face. He looked confused and could it be . . . disappointed?

I got dressed slowly, taking my sweet time. It was the last class of the day so I had nowhere to be. When I left the locker room, I checked to see if the coast was clear. Uh-oh. Hamilton was still there! But then I realized he was deep in conversation with Ashley. He looked pretty serious. I opened the door and sidled out. He didn't even notice me. I told myself I didn't care and headed to my locker.

But I did care. Just a little.

That night after dinner, I told my family what Amy had said that morning.

"I-I don't know what to say," said Mom, blinking in confusion. "A whole school full of kids who don't like flowers?"

Aster, Rose, and Poppy looked puzzled. I knew how they felt. When your family has been in the flower business as long as ours, when a vase of fresh cut flowers on the table is a staple, like milk in the refrigerator, you just don't get it when someone says they don't like flowers. Some people don't like cats. I may not agree, but I get it.

Some people don't like broccoli. This I understand. But flowers? It's like saying you don't like sunshine. Or chocolate cake. Or babies, for heaven's sake.

"So the question is," I said, trying to keep our conversation on track, "how *do* we make flowers for the prom cool?"

"How about using fruit?" suggested Dad. "Like your centerpieces?"

Mom shook her head. "Too messy. One slow dance and there's fruit salad squashed all over the front of someone's tuxedo."

That made me laugh, in spite of everything.

"How about using exotic flowers?" said Rose. "Like . . . birds of paradise!"

"Or hibiscus," said Aster.

I was impressed that my sisters could name exotic flowers. They had definitely been paying attention at the store.

Mom frowned. "Even if we use the most amazing exotic flowers, I don't think that's going to make prom flowers seem cool," she said. "It's still a wrist corsage on an elastic band, you know?"

Nobody knew what to say. So instead, we moved to

the family room and watched two episodes of *Cash Cab*. We yelled out answers, but other than that, we didn't talk.

When it was over, Mom yawned. "Delly?" she said.

"Yes?" I said warily. She always calls me that when she wants me to do something she thinks I won't be interested in doing.

"Would you mind reading to Poppy before bedtime? Daddy and I are really tired tonight."

I sighed. I was just about to ask why Rose or Aster couldn't do it, but the look of excitement on Poppy's face kept my mouth shut. "Sure," I said.

Upstairs, I rifled through the books on Poppy's bookshelf as she brushed her teeth and washed her face, and got changed into a ruffled pink nightgown. She had so many of my old favorites. *Harry the Dirty Dog. Charlotte's Web. Ruby the Copycat. Pippi Longstocking. Ramona the Pest.* Then I spotted an old battered copy of *Alice's Adventures in Wonderland*. Poppy had been disappointed when she hadn't been allowed to see the Tim Burton version, so I thought she might get a kick out of reading the real thing.

"What about this?" I asked as Poppy sat down heavily

on the rug and began peeling off her socks. She always saved them for last.

"Cool," she said. She climbed into bed and pulled the covers up to her chin.

I sat on the edge of her bed, opened the book, and began to read the first chapter. "'Alice was beginning to get very tired of sitting by her sister on the bank, and of having nothing to do . . .'" Right away I could feel Poppy relaxing as the story caught her attention.

I read on. "'. . . So she was considering in her own mind (as well as she could, for the hot day made her feel very sleepy and stupid), whether the pleasure of making a daisy-chain would be worth the trouble of getting up and picking the daisies, when suddenly a White Rabbit with pink eyes — '"

Poppy stopped me. "A daisy chain!" she said, all interested. "What's a daisy chain?"

I laughed in disbelief. Only a Bloom would be more interested in a daisy chain than a white rabbit with pink eyes!

I hadn't made one in years, so I scrunched up my face as I tried to remember how to do it. "Well, you pick a bunch of daisies and make a slit in the stem and thread them all together, until you have a circle. If it's a small circle you have a bracelet, or if it's bigger you can wear it as a crown or even around your neck," I explained. I sighed. "Look, Poppy, if you want me to finish the chapter before bedtime we have to keep going." I was thinking longingly of my own book, waiting for me on my bedside table.

Poppy sat bolt upright in bed. "I want to make a daisy chain!" she said.

"Fine, fine," I said distractedly.

"And then you can wear it as a necklace to the dance at your school!"

"Thanks, Poppy," I said. I smiled, picturing myself in a formal dress and fancy shoes with a chain of daisies around my neck. And then I thought about it again and my mouth fell open. "That's it, Poppy! You're amazing!"

"I am?" Poppy said.

I jumped up and ran to the top of the stairs. "Mom, Dad, come here!"

Mom and Dad quickly ran up the stairs. Rose and Aster were right behind them. Buster, barking away, bounded up the stairs, too.

Mom looked relieved that we were okay. "Did Poppy

decorate the mirror with shaving cream again?" asked my dad warily as everyone joined us in Poppy's room.

"No, I'm amazing!" Poppy exclaimed, bouncing on her bed.

"Tell us, Poppy!" exclaimed Mom.

Poppy turned to me, confused. "Del, how am I amazing again?"

I laughed. "Poppy wants to make me a daisy chain to wear to the middle school prom," I told them.

Everyone just stared at me.

"So the reason none of the high school kids are ordering flowers is that they don't think corsages are cool. But how cool would a necklace of flowers be? Or a . . ."

"Bracelet!" said Rose, looking at me admiringly.

"A ring!" said Aster.

Mom was nodding, a big smile on her face. "This *could* work!" she said. She thought for a moment. "We could really be different — add sequins, feathers, beads. . . . We can go crazy at the craft store tomorrow. Then we can experiment in the afternoon when we're all at the store," she said excitedly. "Great idea, Poppy! Thanks."

"And thanks to you, too, Del," said Dad, putting his

arm around me. "This is a family that knows how to work together!" he added proudly.

Poppy beamed. I did, too. I was more than happy to bask in my family's gratitude for a while longer, but Poppy wanted to get back to Wonderland. "Del — Alice!" she said, pointing to the book. My family said good night and filed out, and I went back to where we had left off. But the whole time my mind was racing with new possibilities for flower necklaces, rings, and bracelets. I couldn't wait to get started.

I was back in my own bed, still excited, when my phone dinged with a text message. It was from Heather. And the news was not good.

I HEARD H. ASKED A. TO THE DANCE AFTER SCHOOL 2DAY.

So that was why Ashley and Hamilton had been talking so seriously after gym class! My heart sank down to my toes. I took a deep breath and texted back a breezy response: GOOD. NOW I DON'T HAVE TO AVOID HIM ANYMORE!

But I didn't feel breezy at all. I felt positively sick about it.

Chapter Seven

The next morning as Mom and I walked to the store, I didn't feel much like talking.

I had sent Becky a simple text late last night: GOT BAD NEWS. CALL ME ASAP IN AM. Becky sometimes liked to sleep in on Saturdays, but I hoped I'd hear from her soon. But part of me was worried that I wouldn't.

"I think you did it again, Del," Mom was saying. "This is exactly what we need to stand out from the competition and convince the high school kids that flowers are cool." She smiled. "Plus, all of us creating designs in the store together today is going to be a lot of fun!"

I nodded. I thought she hadn't noticed my silence, but moms don't seem to miss much — especially when you want them to. When we got to Fairfield Avenue, she turned to me. "Penny for your thoughts," she said.

I shook my head. "I'm fine, Mom. Really."

But Mom did not look convinced.

I bit my lip. How could I possibly tell my mother I was upset because the son of our competitor had asked my arch-nemesis to the school dance? I wasn't even sure where to begin, so I just didn't say anything.

It doesn't matter, I told myself. *I didn't want to go with him, anyway.* But still, the news smarted, like a paper cut on your finger. Just when you've forgotten about it, you move your hand the wrong way and it hurts just as much as when you first got it.

When we reached the store, Mom asked me to get things ready. She would do all the outgoing orders while Dad, Poppy, Aster, and Rose went to the craft store to pick up the supplies. I felt a twinge of excitement as I thought about reinventing the prom corsage. This was just what I needed to get my mind off my middle school prom woes.

At the store, Becky finally called and I told her the whole story. "Oh, Del," she said with a sigh. "I'm sorry." No

"What did you expect?" or "If you had only listened to me." I hung up, feeling better just having talked to her.

By the time Dad and my sisters walked into Petal Pushers, each clutching a bulging bag from Creative Crafts, the store was ready. I had cleared off the worktable (and organized all of Mom's tools, which had been left in a big, messy pile the night before). One by one Dad, Rose, Aster, and Poppy dumped their materials onto the table. Mom squealed with delight as she sifted through the stuff they had bought. Feathers. Glue guns. Snap bracelets. Beads. Jewels. Sequins. And more.

I held up a small black spider. "I can guess who picked this one out," I said.

Aster laughed.

We all stood around the table, eyeing all the craft stuff. Nobody wanted to go first. I wondered if everyone felt the way I did — overwhelmed by our task and intimidated at being creative on demand.

But then Mom got the ball rolling. She plugged in the glue guns and carefully chose an assortment of flowers from the cooler, placing the shears next to them.

"Now, Poppy," she warned. "One of us will help you with these, okay?"

Poppy sighed. "Fine," she said grumpily. I gave her a sympathetic grin. I remembered what it was like when no one trusted you to use sharp things by yourself.

Mom glued pink gerbera daisies, a cluster of purple jewels, and some lighter pink feathers onto a snap bracelet. After allowing it to dry a bit, she snapped it onto Rose's wrist.

We all stared in amazement. Finally, I spoke. "That is the coolest wrist corsage ever, Mom."

"Nice work, Daisy," said Dad.

"I want one, too!" cried Poppy. Rose generously took off the bracelet and snapped it around Poppy's tiny wrist. Poppy beamed up at her sister.

Aster had bought some black spray paint and went into the back to color some daisies. Then, with some help from Mom, she made a very traditional wrist corsage — except for the all-black flowers, and the loops of thin, red ribbons with the tiny skull beads threaded on them. Her eyes were shining as she admired her goth creation.

Rose, not to be outdone by her twin, took single sweetheart roses and glued them in a row onto a wide white ribbon, interspersing them with tiny rhinestones. When she tied it around her neck, we all gasped. Simple and gorgeous.

With Dad's help, Poppy created a pretty corsage of lilacs and some ribbon. She pinned it onto her velvet evening bag and admired it. "Look at my beautiful purse corsage," she said solemnly. "I am a great idea-er."

We all agreed, with straight faces, that she was indeed a great idea-er.

Mom took the elastic out of her hair and glued a big gerbera daisy on it. "Del, come here," she said with a smile. I felt like a little kid again as she gathered my hair into a ponytail and wrapped the elastic around it. She held up a hand mirror and I admired my new hair corsage. I couldn't help but wonder if Hamilton would like the way it looked . . . but then I pushed the thought away.

Dad avoided all the girly stuff by making a collection of boutonnieres with all sorts of different flowers — bluebells, one of Aster's black daisies, even a sunflower! Not a rose or carnation in sight.

And me? I made a collection of totally serviceable snap bracelet corsages. I stared at them. Nothing really stood out as amazing. If you haven't figured it out yet, I can be a bit of a perfectionist. I was pretty disappointed in myself that my flowers weren't the best of the bunch.

"I wish I had my camera," Mom said. "Then we could remember exactly how to re-create everything."

I realized I could take pictures with the camera on my phone, so I started snapping away. Rose modeled her namesake necklace. Aster held her skull corsage up proudly. Mom tried on one of Poppy's ring corsages and held up her hand, admiring it. "We are an amazing creative team!" she said happily. "The kids are going to go crazy for our designs."

"Hey, I think someone's here now!" screeched Poppy. I looked up. She was right; someone was loitering outside the door.

Not wanting a possible customer to get away, I hurried over to the door and pushed it open. "Welcome to . . ."

My voice trailed off as I stood blinking in the sunlight at our "customer." Tall. Cute. Sandy-haired. It was Hamilton Baldwin.

What was he *doing* here?

He smiled at me, his dimple showing. "Hey, Del," he said. "I heard you worked here on weeken —"

Quickly, I stepped outside, shutting the door behind me. My heart was hammering.

"What are you doing here?" I hissed.

"I came by to say hello, since we never seem to get a chance to talk at school!" he said with a grin.

My mind was racing a million miles an hour. Proms. Ashley. Fleur. Our new designs. Suddenly, I knew exactly what Hamilton was up to — since Fleur wasn't getting any prom business, either, his mom must have sent him here to see what *we* were working on!

This was completely unacceptable! I spread my arms out wide across the store window, hoping to block his view of the goings-on inside. Since Hamilton's at least six inches taller than me, I am pretty sure my oh-so-cool maneuver didn't work.

"You can't be here," I said. I glared at him, furious at his brazenness.

His eyes widened. "Oh, does your boss get mad when friends come by?" He frowned. "I'm sorry."

My boss? So he was playing dumb. "Yeah," I said tersely. "My boss doesn't like it when people come snooping around."

Hamilton looked at me quizzically. "Snooping?" he asked. "You seem a little stressed out, Del. Is everything okay?"

I just stared at him. I couldn't believe he was trying to distract me with the nice-guy act. Well, I was onto him!

"Okay, I'll go," said Hamilton, backing up a few paces. "I just wanted to ask you a question first."

"Fine," I said. Whatever it took to get rid of him.

"So what's this I hear about Bob?" he said. "Is it true that you guys are really . . . you know . . . ?" He trailed off.

I looked at him like he was crazy. Why was he asking if Bob the Bully and I were really lab partners? Why did he care? What a weirdo!

"Yeah, it's true," I said hastily. "Is that it?"

"It is?" said Hamilton. He looked at me closely. "I just don't get it. I'm sorry, but he's such a . . . jerk."

I shrugged. "Like I had a choice?"

Now Hamilton looked really confused. His brow wrinkled. "You didn't have a choice?" he asked.

"It was assigned," I explained with a sigh.

He gave me a blank look.

"By our teacher," I clarified.

Hamilton opened his mouth as if he were going to ask me another question. But nothing came out. He shut his mouth and frowned.

Just then Poppy poked her head out of the door. "Del!" she called. "Wait till you see, come quick! Aster just made a . . ."

I shook my head as crazily as Buster does when he's playing with one of his squeaky toys. "I'll be there in a minute, Poppy!" I shouted frantically before she could spill the beans. "Go back inside. Right now!" Poppy stuck out her tongue at me. But she listened. I turned back to Hamilton. "I've got to get back to work," I told him.

Hamilton let out a long sigh. "Okay. Bye, Del," he said somewhat sadly.

Without giving him another glance, I marched back inside. The bell rang, mocking me with its merry tone. I was officially ticked off.

"Look at this, Del!" Aster said, holding up a double ring corsage. She'd glued two plastic rings together and covered them with tiny flowers and sparkling jewels. It was seriously cool looking, but I was still seething.

"Who came by just now?" Dad asked, glancing out the door.

"Oh, just some kid I know from school," I replied through gritted teeth. "Not a customer. At all."

"Hey, honey," Mom said, not noticing my anger. She held up my phone. "Let me take a picture of the ponytail holder."

I turned around so she could get a good angle, and realized with horror that I'd worn it in front of Hamilton. Had he noticed it? Would he report back to his mother? Would she steal our cool idea?

How stupid of me! I couldn't believe I had ever been interested in a blatant spy like Hamilton Baldwin.

The war had escalated. Hamilton had gone behind enemy lines. It was time to counterstrike.

Chapter Eight

I realized there was only one way to find out what Hamilton had learned from his spy mission. I would spy right back. It was only fair, right? And I would do it alone, I decided, remembering my last spying mission with Becky. She had cracked under pressure, big-time.

I couldn't tell Mom the truth, because then I would have to explain about Hamilton. And I just wasn't ready for that yet. So the next day, I asked for a ride to the mall, saying that I needed to go shopping for the prom.

Mom smiled. "Oh good," she said. "Dad and I have some errands to run today and I wasn't sure what we were going to do with Poppy."

I shook my head. I did not want to take my five-year-old sister on a top-secret spying mission! But Mom was firm — if I didn't take Poppy, I was not going to the mall. End of story.

So that's how my five-year-old sister and I ended up being spies together.

"Now, this is a secret," I told her once Mom had dropped us off with strict instructions to meet her at the south entrance at four o'clock. "A special, oldest sister–littlest sister secret we have to keep for a while."

Poppy nodded solemnly. "Keep it secret. Check!" she said. She reached into her evening bag and pulled out a notebook and a pen. "I'll take notes," she told me.

I rolled my eyes. Poppy doesn't know how to write yet.

"Okay," I whispered. "They don't know you at Fleur. But I've been here before. I don't want to be recognized, so I'll have to wear a disguise." I reached into my shoulder bag and pulled out a floppy hat and a pair of sunglasses.

Poppy scribbled some jagged shapes in her notebook. "Disguises. Check!" Then she looked at me. "I definitely need a disguise, too," she said.

When I told her she actually didn't need one, her lower lip began to tremble. I looked around wildly. A sporting goods store was nearby. Five minutes later I was ten bucks poorer and Poppy was wearing a fishing cap.

Poppy gave me a big grin. "I like spying with you, Del," she said.

"Good. Now remember, you can't call me by name."

She nodded and scribbled in her notebook again. "Don't call Del Del," she said. "Check!"

"Here goes nothing," I said. I grabbed Poppy by the hand, plastered a smile on my face, and walked briskly toward the store entrance.

"Welcome to Fleur," said Hamilton's mom as she stepped out from behind the counter. I took a close look at her. Her blonde hair was pulled back into a neat bun. She was pretty, with perfectly applied makeup. She had fine lines around her eyes, which were a brilliant shade of blue. Just like Hamilton's.

Poppy looked around at the vast space, her eyes wide. "Wow, what a beautiful store," she said.

I gave her a dirty look behind my sunglasses.

"Why, thank you. And what's your name, little girl?" Hamilton's mom asked, bending her knees so she could look at Poppy's face. "What a cute hat."

I stiffened. What would she say?

"Um . . . Mercedes," replied Poppy. "My name is Mercedes."

I stared at my little sister. Where did *that* come from?

"Hello, Mercedes," Hamilton's mom said. She turned to me. "And you're . . ."

"Gertrude!" Poppy answered.

Gertrude? I didn't want to be Gertrude!

"Gertrude, do you go to Sarah Hale Middle School?" she asked. "Maybe you know my son, Hamilton."

I totally panicked. "We'd better start shopping!" I said, grabbing Poppy's hand and dragging her down the orchid aisle. I mentally urged Hamilton's mom to go about her business so I could hopefully overhear some info and get out of there ASAP. I glanced around nervously. If Hamilton showed up, the jig would certainly be up.

Hamilton's mom shrugged and returned to her place behind the counter.

"Mercedes," I said in a louder than usual voice, "do you like this orchid for Mom's birthday?"

"Mom's birthday isn't until December, silly," said Poppy, matching my volume. I gave her the hairy eyeball. "Oh. I mean, I love it for Mom's birthday. Yes, I do."

Just then the door whooshed open. I froze, but then

saw it was a tall, middle-aged woman — not Hamilton. Whew. I put my finger to my lips and Poppy and I eavesdropped.

"Hi, Nancy," said Hamilton's mom. "How are things at Children's Closet?"

"Pretty good," said Nancy. "We just had a big sale and we turned over a lot of merchandise. How are things here?"

Score!

"Not getting that prom business I had been anticipating," Hamilton's mom said.

Poppy and I exchanged a meaningful glance.

"Oh, I'm sorry to hear that," said Nancy. "What do you think you'll do about it?"

"I just came up with a great idea," said Hamilton's mom. "Totally creative. It's going to get those tweens and teens lining up outside the door."

My mouth fell open. What nerve! The only reason she had a great idea was thanks to me and my family. I had heard enough. My worst fears had been confirmed. I grabbed Poppy by the arm and dragged her out of the store.

"Good-bye, Mercedes! Good-bye, Gertrude!" called Hamilton's mom.

"Good-bye," I said icily over my shoulder as we headed out the door.

Once we were outside, Poppy straightened her cap. "Well, she seemed like a really nice lady," she said.

We had another hour before Mom picked us up, so Poppy and I wandered the mall, window-shopping. My heart wasn't in it. I could only think about Hamilton's mom stealing our ideas. And since kids hung out in the mall all the time, she was definitely going to win the prom battle. All she had to do was fill her front window with all of our cool creations.

When Poppy complained that she was hungry, I got her a box of popcorn from the Snack Shack and we sat down at a table nearby. Idly, I glanced at a group of older girls sitting at a table in front of the Wok and Roll. They were laughing loudly, drinking sodas, and sharing one order of French fries. I took a closer look at one of the girls. It was Amber, Amy's big sister!

She was very pretty, with long, thick, reddish brown hair the same color as Amy's. When she spoke, the other girls seemed to hang on her every word. They laughed at all her jokes. I noticed that she was wearing a pair of black motorcycle boots and had a bandanna pulled through her jeans loops like a belt. Then I took a closer look. At least three of the girls in her group were sporting the exact same look. *Interesting,* I thought. It reminded me of the time that Ashley Edwards had accidentally spilled orange paint all over her black shirt in art class, and the next day three girls showed up with deliberately paint-splattered clothes.

That's when it hit me: Popular girls set trends. Sometimes even accidentally! And just as suddenly, I knew exactly what I needed to do.

"I'll be right back," I said to Poppy. "I'm going to talk to that girl over there. To convince her to come to Petal Pushers."

Poppy shrugged and put a huge handful of popcorn into her mouth. Now that she had her snack, she didn't care about anything else.

I was a little nervous. I took a deep breath and marched over to Amber and her friends. They didn't look up.

"Um, hi, Amber," I said.

No response. I licked my lips and tried again.

I cleared my throat. "Um, Amber . . ." I said.

A silence fell over the chattering girls. And then they swiveled around and stared at me. Yikes.

"Hey, Amber," I said. "Remember me? I'm friends with your sister, Amy. . . ." my voice trailed off.

Amber looked up at me. "Are you kidding me? No middle school kids allowed," she said. "Get lost."

As I stood there, wanting to melt into the floor, the rest of the girls all burst out laughing.

Chapter Nine

My face fell. Complete and total humiliation!

Just then Amber jumped up. She reached out to put a hand on my arm. "Oh, Del, I'm just kidding!" She laughed, and then so did the rest of the girls. "I'm so sorry," she added. "I just couldn't resist."

"Um . . . okay," I replied, not sure what to say. Was that supposed to be funny? Because it so totally was not.

"Are you looking for Amy?" Amber asked, smiling warmly. "She's at home."

"Actually, I wanted to talk to you," I said. "Do you have a minute?"

She gave me a funny look, then shrugged. "Sure," she said. We walked over to the fountain and sat on the edge. I could keep my eye on Poppy, who was still scarfing down handfuls of popcorn. I looked down and saw a thick carpet of pennies and nickels that shoppers had thrown into the fountain. *That's an awful lot of wishes,* I thought.

Amber stared at me expectantly. "So what's up?" she asked.

"It's about the prom," I said. "You know my family owns a flower shop, right?" I asked.

"Right," said Amber. "Your grandparents did my bat mitzvah flowers. They were really nice."

"That's great." I took a deep breath. "I need to ask you a favor."

"Oh yeah?" said Amber warily.

I soldiered on. "I know that the high school kids aren't getting corsages this year for the prom," I said.

"That's right," Amber said. "Nobody wants those lame orchid wrist corsages." She made a face. "So grandma, you know?"

"I know," I said. "That's why we've created this line of cool prom flowers."

Amber looked skeptical. I reached into my bag and pulled out my phone. I flipped it open and pressed a bunch of buttons until I found my photos.

"This is a gerbera-daisy-and-feather-snap-bracelet corsage," I said. Amber leaned in closely, then took the phone from my hand.

She looked up at me. "Wow," she said. "That *is* really beautiful."

The next picture was of Rose's rose-and-rhinestone choker.

"That's gorgeous!" said Amber. "Huh," she said, looking puzzled. "I had no idea prom flowers could be so cool."

I bit my lip. "So do you think maybe you and your friends would come by the store to check them out?"

"Definitely!" she said. "Is tomorrow after cheerleading good? Around five thirty?"

"Perfect," I said. "Thanks, Amber!"

"Thank *you*!" she replied. "Oh, and um . . . sorry about before."

I looked at her.

"About pretending I didn't know you."

"Oh that," I said. "No problem!" But I resolved that I would always be nice to my little sisters' friends.

"How'd it go?" asked Poppy as I joined her at the table.

"Great!" I said. "Amber and her cheerleader friends are coming to the store tomorrow to check out the flowers!"

"Gertrude, that's great!" she said, grinning at me. She opened up her notebook. "Talk to cheerleaders. Check!"

As we headed to the south entrance to meet Mom, I felt like I was walking on air. So what if I hadn't made the prettiest prom flowers in my family? I was a creative businessperson. My expertise was bringing in the customers. It didn't matter how pretty the product was if you didn't have anyone to buy it.

The whole family had come to pick us up. We were going to get takeout, ice cream, and a movie for our new Sunday night tradition.

As Poppy and I got in the car, I thought for a moment about how to most dramatically break the news.

"The cheerleaders are coming to the store to buy corsages!" Poppy announced.

Oh well.

Mom spun around in her seat. "Really, Del?" she asked. "How'd you pull that one off?"

After I told them what had happened with Amber,

they were so happy they even let me pick out the ice-cream flavor. Rocky Road, of course.

That night, after we had eaten our sundaes, we decided to iChat with Gran and Gramps before the movie. The news was too exciting not to share right away.

We were so happy to see Gran's and Gramps's tanned, relaxed faces that we all started talking at once.

"Let Del tell it," said Dad.

So I told them everything. Okay, not *everything* everything. I couldn't really discuss Hamilton. I also left out the spying. And luckily Poppy did, too.

"How funny," said Gran. "You never know what those high school kids will think of next. Flowers being old-fashioned — how silly! Well, it sounds like you guys are fixing that. I'm really proud of you all."

I could feel myself relax just hearing Gran's voice. Once we had caught up on the Key West news, which involved fishing tournaments and a visit to an underwater hotel, Rose had an important question.

"So, tell us about *your* prom, Gran," she said.

Gran giggled. "Well, my date was the handsomest boy in the whole school. . . ." she began.

"That's right," said Gramps. "Me!"

"It was our first date," Gran continued. "He told me later he'd been wanting to ask me out all school year and finally got up his nerve to ask me to the prom." She laughed. "His face was so red!"

Gramps smiled. "She was the prettiest and smartest girl in the school," he said.

Gran blushed. "I was so excited, I bought the most beautiful dress I could find. And I also had the nicest flowers, of course. Gramps came in to Flowers on Fairfield early to order them, and my father went all out."

"It's nice to hear a happy prom story," I said. "Mom's and Dad's were kind of sad."

"I got a four point four," Dad protested. We all ignored him.

"I have another sad prom story for you," said Gran. She lowered her voice. "Your Great-aunt Lily didn't have a very nice evening at all."

"That's right," said Mom, remembering.

"What happened?" Aster asked.

"She went with the captain of the football team. He was very sure of himself, and very self-centered," Gran explained. "He completely forgot to order her a corsage! When he showed up at the house empty-handed, my father put together a corsage out of the flowers we had in the house. Imagine that — the daughter of the town florist had the worst flowers at the prom. Lily was so embarrassed."

"Wow," I said. That *was* a sad story. But it felt weird to feel sorry for mean Aunt Lily.

"Well, we don't mean to end our conversation on such a down note," said Gramps. "This is great news. Give us a call and let us know how it all goes."

"Will do, Dad," said Mom.

After a chorus of love yous and miss yous and talk to you soons, we disconnected. I stared at the blank computer screen sadly.

"Let's go watch our movie now!" said Mom. "I don't want you girls staying up too late. Tomorrow's a big day."

It most certainly would be. We had pulled ahead in the battle. Now we had to make our final charge.

Chapter Ten

When I arrived at the store on Monday afternoon, I saw that Mom had been busy. Mom spends most of her Mondays making the arrangements for Oscar's, the fanciest restaurant in town, but she had found the time to re-create all of the prom flowers, too. (I'd left her my phone with the photos for reference.) And she had done an amazing job. They looked perfect.

Mom had also brought in hand mirrors and a table mirror so the girls would be able to admire themselves. She even bought some sodas and set out bowls of snacks. I grabbed a handful of pretzels and started munching.

"A party!" said Rose as she pushed open the door to the store. Rose, who was ten going on sixteen as Gran liked to say, wasn't going to miss a gathering of high school girls for the world. She turned to Aster, who walked in right after her. "Doesn't this get you all excited for our sleepover on Saturday night?"

"Sure does," replied Aster cheerily. I stared at her in disbelief. Was she for real?

"Now promise me you won't wear black. And you'll let me put some lip gloss on you."

Aster sighed. "Sure, Rosie."

I gazed at my sisters. Maybe Rose was right. Maybe Aster *was* looking forward to going to this party. Stranger things had happened, I guessed.

We had just set out the last bowl of chips when Amber and her entourage arrived. Ten chatty, giggling, shiny-lipped, sleek-haired girls.

There was a whole lot of oohing and ahhing over the designs as the girls tried them on. They switched flowers with each other, showed Mom pictures of their dresses that they had on their phones, and consulted with her about which flowers would look the best. Mom was flushed and laughing as she took down notes.

Soon enough, the girls got down to business: choosing the corsages that their dates would pick up for them.

"Jonathan is going to be totally relieved — he doesn't

have to do any work!" said a bubbly, blonde girl.

A girl with short, black hair laughed. "Except pick it up and pay for it!" she said.

The blonde girl grinned. "Yeah, I forgot about that part!"

The bell above the door rang as an even bigger group of girls pushed their way inside.

I felt a swell of happiness. I turned to Amber. "Are these friends of yours, too?"

She shrugged. "I tweeted about Petal Pushers," she said. "I have a lot of followers, you know. I'm cohead cheerleader."

"Oh, I know," I said with a grin.

Mom waved to me gaily from across the store.

I waved back. Prom season was saved!

A couple of hours later, the last girl left the store. We dumped out half-eaten bowls of snacks and rinsed out soda cans for recycling.

Mom locked the front door. "That was great." She sighed. "I'm totally exhausted! But happy." She looked at me. "Hey, I just thought of something. Should I make corsages for you and Becky?"

"That's a great idea," I said. "I'm not sure what color dress she's wearing, though." I texted my BFF right away.

WRIST CORSAGE 4 DANCE? I wrote. I snapped my phone shut.

"Okay, let me know when you hear from her," said Mom. "And you?"

"Surprise me," I said. "I'm going to wear my light blue dress." It was the only fancy dress I had and I hauled it out for all occasions — recitals, holidays, etc. I had made the decision not to buy anything new. I was just going to keep Becky company, after all.

The next morning I filled in my friends about how great everything had gone.

"It's true!" said Amy. "Amber was going on and on about how cool the flowers are!" She nodded wisely. "And there will be more middle school orders coming in, now that it's cool with the high school kids."

"Your sister is great," I said. "She really came through for us."

Amy smiled. "She *is* great," she said. "Most of the time, anyway." Then she sighed.

"What's wrong, Amy?" I asked. But I knew what was wrong.

"Brian still hasn't asked me," she said sadly.

"Looks like you'll be going stag with me and Becky," I told her.

She gave me a hangdog look.

"Hey!" I said. "We'll have fun!"

Heather looked at Amy sympathetically. "I feel guilty being so excited when you're so disappointed," she told her. Then she brightened. "But Billy and I are going to have such an amazing time!"

Jessica grinned. "Yeah, me and Jackson, too."

Amy sighed again.

"Cheer up," I said. "There are way worse things." I glanced up just as Bob and Matt passed by our table. Bob gave me a dirty look.

"You could be going with Bob," I said in a low voice, so they couldn't hear me. "Or his lame twin, Matt."

Everyone laughed. Everyone that is, but Becky. She looked down at the table.

"Hey, you never got back to me about the corsage

question," I said to her. "Do you want my mom to make you one?"

Becky froze. She stared at the table and wouldn't meet my eyes. "I . . . I think maybe I won't need one," she said.

"Are you sure?" I asked. I whipped out my phone, about to show her the pictures. "They're really beautiful."

"No, it's okay, Del," replied Becky.

I frowned at her. Why was she being so difficult? She knew this prom flower thing was a big deal for me. And she was usually so supportive. I looked at her searchingly. But she didn't look up. Annoyed, I decided to drop it.

"So what are the chances of Brian asking me to the dance, do you think?" Amy asked brightly. "Slim to none or a definite possibility?"

We all groaned.

Four days and counting until this prom madness was officially over!

Chapter Eleven

I searched for Becky after school to see if she wanted to walk home together, but couldn't find her anywhere. When I left the building, I was surprised to find her waiting outside, looking impatient.

"Hey, Becky," I said.

"Oh hey, Del," she said nervously.

"What are you doing?" I asked. "Waiting for your mom?"

"Yeah," she said.

"And where are you going?" I prodded.

Was it my imagination or did my best friend look uncomfortable? "To the . . . mall," she finally answered.

"For what?" I asked curiously.

She looked up at the sky. "I thought I'd look for a prom dress," she said softly.

"Without me?" I said with a grin. "Well, it sounds like fun. Mind if I come along?"

"Are you sure?" asked Becky. "I thought you said you had a mountain of Spanish homework."

"Finished it in study hall," I said. "I'll text my mom right now. I'm sure she'll be fine with it."

"O-okay," said Becky.

Becky's mom pulled up a couple of minutes later in her shiny red car and we climbed into the backseat.

"Buckle up, girls," said Mrs. Davis, looking crisp and professional in a pin-striped suit. "This is exciting! Your first formal dance. With fancy dresses and dates and all that fun stuff."

I laughed. "No dates for us," I told her. "Becky and I are going stag."

"That's right," Becky said quickly.

When we arrived at the mall, Mrs. Davis handed Becky her credit card and said she'd be working on her laptop in the food court if we needed her.

We went straight to Fashions by Fiona. Becky is a careful shopper, and takes her time. I had no money and my mom had certainly not given me *her* credit card, so I just picked a few things to try on for fun. A pair of studded jeans. A fake fur vest. A red sequined dress. I thought I'd make Becky laugh.

But Becky was taking her dress shopping very seriously. She barely smiled as I struck a silly pose in the shiny dress. "What do you think?" she asked, modeling a black dress with pink flowers.

I looked her up and down. "It's a little short," I told her. "If you dropped something, you might be afraid to bend over and pick it up!"

But Becky didn't even crack a smile. She looked at her reflection and nodded. "I'll be right back," she said.

A white dress with puffy sleeves looked too little-girl. A shiny black dress was pretty, but had a plunging neckline. "Your mom will kill you!" I said.

Several changes later, Becky came out of the dressing room in the perfect dress. It was a soft pink that looked gorgeous against her dark skin. With an empire waist, a full skirt, and cap sleeves, it fit like it was made for her.

Becky looked pleased as she studied herself in the mirror, a faint smile stealing over her face.

"Oh, Becky," I breathed. "You look gorgeous."

Her purchase was wrapped in tissue paper and placed in a bright pink bag. I assumed we'd head to the food court to meet her Mom. But no. Becky wanted to find the perfect pair of shoes.

"Where is my friend Becky and what have you done with her?" I joked as we headed to the shoe store. I'd suggested we take the long way around so we wouldn't have to pass by Fleur. After the last time, I didn't want to take any chances that Hamilton's mom would recognize me. She might think I was a stalker or something!

Becky smiled sheepishly. "I know I'm not usually the girliest girl," she said. "But this is kind of fun." She smiled. "I'm glad you came with me, Del."

By the end of the shopping spree, Becky had purchased a pair of pretty silver flats, a delicate silver necklace with a heart charm, and small silver hoops.

"You've upped the ante," I said to Becky. "My old blue dress isn't going to cut it anymore." I laughed. "I'm impressed that you're going all out just for me!"

I waited for her to laugh. But Becky just bit her lip and looked at me as if she was going to say something. But she didn't.

Wednesday afternoon. The school day was done. I had somehow managed to miss seeing Bob, Ashley, *and* Hamilton. An avoidance trifecta!

I packed up my books quickly, threw my bag over my shoulder, and slipped out the side door, which is rarely used because it locks behind you. No getting back inside unless you go around the block to the front entrance. Normally, this wouldn't be an issue for me. But that day it was. Just my luck — it had just started to pour.

Sheets of rain lashed down from the sky, and the sidewalk was already running with rivers of water. And I had no umbrella, no raincoat, no nothing. My heart sank as I pressed myself against the metal door to avoid getting wet. If I ran around to the front entrance, I'd get soaked. I sighed. I'd have to wait it out. Either the rain would stop or someone else would come out the side entrance and I could get back inside.

The wind changed direction and I started to get pelted with rain. An image of myself on the living room couch, a cup of hot cocoa in one hand and a book in the other made me sigh with longing.

I had just started shivering when I heard the delightful sound of the heavy metal door creaking open. I smiled, ready to thank my savior. I'd be back inside in no time. "Hold . . ." I started to say, but then my voice trailed off.

The person who had opened the door was Hamilton. He, of course, held an umbrella in his hand.

I was too shocked to ask him to hold the door for me. We stared at each other as it slammed shut behind him. Great. Now I was stuck huddling outside in the rain — with the person I least wanted to see. Can you say *awkward*?

Hamilton cleared his throat. "Del, I've been wanting to apologize to you," he said.

"What you did was wrong," I said, unable to make eye contact with him. I felt a steely hard anger inside me.

Wait a minute, I thought. *Are you more mad because of the spying — or because of Ashley?* I wasn't sure and that made me feel even angrier.

I glanced up at the sky. Could I make a run for it? No, the rain was getting even worse.

Hamilton stared at his sneakers, then looked up. "But I just can't apologize," he said slowly. "I think I was right!"

I turned to him as a big, fat, cold raindrop fell on my head. "You're right?" I sputtered. "How could you be right?"

"It just doesn't make sense," he said.

I looked at him, puzzled. Now what was *that* supposed to mean? *He* didn't make any sense. I thrust my hands in my pockets and turned away. "You shouldn't have done it," I told him.

"I know," he replied. With a sigh, he pulled his sweatshirt hood over his head.

"Del," he started. "You're making a terrible decision. There — I said it." I stared after him, my mouth open in disbelief as he took off, jumping over puddles as he sprinted down the street. It was official. Hamilton Baldwin was crazy. What was he even talking about?

I waited for a while longer, in the hopes that someone else would come out of the building to let me back in. When no one showed up, I decided it was time to make a run for it, rain or no rain. Just before I left I looked down. And there, on the ground where Hamilton had just been standing, was his umbrella. *He must have forgotten it,* I thought. *Too bad for him.*

But as I walked home, sheltered from the driving rain

by the roomy umbrella, another thought occurred to me. Maybe Hamilton had left the umbrella for me on purpose.

Hamilton got soaking wet so I wouldn't have to.

I gritted my teeth. Why was he making it so hard for me to hate him?

Mom came home that night grinning from ear to ear. Rose, Aster, Poppy, and I had been having a secret discussion in the living room and we stopped talking as soon as she walked in the door.

I gave my sisters a warning look. It said, *Keep your mouths shut.* Rose and Aster nodded.

"What are you guys up to?" asked Mom, sitting on the couch and removing her shoes.

"Homework," I said, although we didn't have any books with us. I hoped she wouldn't notice.

"Planning a . . ." Poppy started to say. Rose quickly put her hand over Poppy's mouth. Luckily, Mom was distracted.

"I was so busy this afternoon!" she said. "I didn't even have a second to sit down!" Dad heard Buster barking joyfully at Mom's return and came in to the room from his study. He sat on the couch next to her, and began to rub her feet.

"More high school kids?" Rose asked.

"Not just high school kids," Mom said with a grin. "Lots more kids from Del's school, too!"

I smiled. Amy had been right.

Mom shook her head. "I was taking down order after order," she said. "There were so many kids coming in I could hardly keep them all straight."

I leaned forward, my eyes wide. "Mom, you have to keep careful records. I hope you remembered to give everyone a receipt!"

Mom laughed. "Relax, Del, I'm just kidding. I was really careful. It was just all a big blur . . . except for this one kid from your school who came in to order a corsage for his date. He was just so sweet and nervous! It nearly broke my heart!"

"I wonder who it was," I said. Then I smiled. "Oh, I bet it's Carmine Belloni. He's going to the dance with his dream girl."

Mom scrunched up her mouth. "No, it wasn't Carmine," she said. "But whoever it was told me he was going to the dance with the smartest and prettiest girl in the school. And the flowers should be extra-special."

"That *is* sweet," I said. I wondered who it could be. Both the nice boy and his smart, pretty date.

"Well, that's exciting," said Rose. "Almost as exciting as the big party we're going to, right, Aster?"

"Right," said Aster, curling her feet underneath her on the sofa.

"I'm thinking that we should both wear these cute pink T-shirts with purple flowers and rhinestones on them," said Rose. "I saw them at the mall. It would be like when we were little and Mom dressed us in matching clothes. Wouldn't that be totally awesome?"

We all turned to look at Aster. She couldn't possibly be excited at the prospect of wearing a pink shirt with purple flowers and rhinestones on it. And matching, no less? But Aster only shrugged. "Awesome," she said.

My parents and I looked at one another, eyebrows raised. Life was certainly full of surprises.

Chapter Twelve

It was Friday, the day before both proms. Everyone at school was buzzing with excitement. I wondered if it was the same at the high school. Doubtful. They were probably too cool for that.

Heather couldn't stop talking about how much fun she was going to have hanging out with Billy Walters and his friends on the soccer team. Jessica was happy to be going with Jackson. And Amy had given up on being asked by Brian, couldn't get up the nerve to ask him herself, and was coming to terms with going stag with Becky and me.

Becky had been surprisingly quiet on the subject. I assumed she was excited to wear her new outfit and have some fun with Amy and me.

I was so happy about the flower orders that I was even looking forward to the prom. Just as long as I avoided seeing Hamilton and Ashley slow dancing together!

I hadn't seen too much of Ashley the past week. I had been expecting her to gloat about going to the dance with Hamilton. But she hadn't said anything about it at all. *Something is very fishy,* I thought.

Luckily, Mom had gotten me out of gym class again to help out with the hundreds of corsages we needed to make that night. So I didn't have to see Ashley or Hamilton that afternoon. I would see enough of them all tomorrow, that was for sure.

My entire family assembled in the store that afternoon and everyone had a great time gluing and designing and arranging. We also mapped out a plan for the next day: We'd get to the store bright and early to do the finishing touches. The only fly in the ointment was that Poppy had a birthday party that afternoon, so Dad would have to leave early to take her. But we'd be fine without them for a couple of hours. Afterward, he and Poppy would come back to the store, so Rose, Aster, and I could go home to get ready for our respective parties, and Mom wouldn't have to be alone.

We closed up and walked home together, joking and laughing. Just as we stepped in the front door of my house, my cell phone rang. It was Amy.

"Hey, Amy," I said. "What's up —"

"Del, I don't know how to tell you this," she said. "I was at the mall tonight getting new shoes for the dance and I saw something . . . weird."

"Weird?" I echoed.

"Very weird," she replied. "I'm just going to come out and say it." She took a deep breath. "IsawBeckywalkingout-ofFleurwithacorsageboxinherhand," she said all in a rush.

"What?" I said. My blood went cold.

"I saw Becky walking out of Fleur with a corsage box in her hand," Amy repeated, more slowly this time.

"That can't be," I finally answered. "Becky said she didn't want a corsage. Plus, she'd never go to Fleur. She's my best friend." I shook my head. "Are you sure it wasn't someone else? Someone who looks like her?" I suggested hopefully.

"So someone who looks just like Becky borrowed her purple Converse high-tops, and turned around when I called her name, and then took off?" Amy asked.

"Yeah," I said, my heart sinking. There was no denying it. My very best friend had betrayed me. But . . . why? Did she like their flowers better? Was she mad at me for some reason? Getting even with me for something I didn't realize I had done? It just didn't make sense. I thought for a moment. She *had* been acting weird lately — not answering her phone, being quieter that usual. What was going on?

"I'm sorry, Del," said Amy. "I'm just telling you what I saw." Then her voice brightened. "Hey, my new shoes are so gorgeous," she said. "Wait till you see them. You want to go over to the dance together tomorrow? You could pick me up on your way."

"Sure," I said distractedly. "See you tomorrow."

I hung up, frozen in disbelief. *Why* had Becky gone to Fleur? Especially without telling me? I tried to remember if there was anything I had done to make her turn on me like this. Nothing made sense.

But I did know one thing — her actions were completely inexcusable.

I flipped open my phone and pressed her number. But it rang and rang with no answer.

"Becky, it's Del," I said when her voice mail picked up. "I heard something weird from Amy. Will you please call me back? I think we need to talk."

I hung up, and waited a whole five minutes, while all around me my family settled in and Dad called Jade Mountain to order Chinese food. When no text or call from Becky came through, I called her again. I could feel myself starting to get flushed with growing anger. Once again, I got her voice mail. Was she *avoiding me*?

"Becky, it's Del again," I said. I paused. "Um . . . so Amy told me you got a corsage at Fleur. I just don't understand why you'd betray me like that. You told me you didn't even want a corsage!" My voice began to get louder. "I thought you were my best friend. But I don't think best friends act this way. I thought we didn't keep secrets from —"

"*BEEP!* If you are finished leaving your message, press one. If you would like to rerecord your message, press two," droned the chipper voice on Becky's phone.

I couldn't believe it! Becky's voice mail had cut me off!

Angrily, I pressed one and slapped my phone shut. I fumed all through dinner with my family, and didn't even enjoy the moo goo gai pan. As I got ready for bed, I kept checking my phone, certain Becky would call me back to explain or apologize. But there was no word from her.

The next morning was crazy busy, which was good — I had less time to dwell on the Becky situation. (She *still* hadn't called me back.) Mom realized we had forgotten to make a dozen boutonnieres, so as soon as we got to the store, we had to rush around to finish them before the middle and high school kids started coming in. I also checked all the corsages to see if they needed any last-minute fixes. When I wasn't hot-glue-gunning errant sequins, I was trying to locate extra corsage boxes, and then lining up the corsages by order number so they'd be easy to locate.

The high school kids came in on their own and seemed pretty cool about everything. Most of the middle school kids came in with their moms and looked a little nervous. It was the first formal dance any of us had ever been to, so I guess it made sense. I smiled and waved to all the kids I knew from my school. Carmine proudly showed me the bluebell wrist corsage he'd picked out. "Look at this, Del," he said. "Penelope told me these are her favorite flowers. She's going to love it!"

"Great, Carmine," I said. And I was happy for him. But I was going through the motions with a heavy heart. I was angry at Becky. That, coupled with the anticipation of having to watch master spy Hamilton and snooty Princess Ashley dance together, was almost too much to think about.

I noticed Mom doing some last-minute tinkering with a snap-on corsage that was so lovely it took my breath away.

Pink and purple hydrangea florets and stephanotises surrounded by delicately gathered tulle, and set on a thick pink ribbon for tying around the wrist. In the middle, perched as if it were in mid-nectar sip, sat a tiny gossamer butterfly. I had never seen anything quite so adorable in my life.

I gave Mom a curious look. She grinned. "I kind of went all out on this one," she said. "I couldn't resist. This is the one for that boy I told you about. The one who is going with the smartest and prettiest girl in your middle school?" She smiled. "I mean the smartest and prettiest girl after *you*, of course!" she added.

"Oh, Mom," I said, shaking my head. What a goofball. I took a closer look at the delicate corsage. "You really outdid yourself," I said.

Mom seemed touched by my compliment. "Thanks, Del," she replied.

"Where is he?" I wondered. "I'm really curious about who this mystery boy is!"

Rose was behind the counter, fidgeting and checking the time on the wall clock. She was raring to start getting ready for the slumber party. I, on the other hand, was perfectly happy to postpone going to the prom indefinitely. But we had to wait for Dad and Poppy to get there. We were keeping the store open an hour late for any last-minute pickups and we all agreed that Mom shouldn't have to handle a rush all by herself.

Rose turned to Aster. "Which pajamas are you planning to wear tonight?" she wanted to know.

Aster shrugged. "My usual," she said.

Rose blanched. "Not that old Smiths T-shirt and the saggy long johns!" she cried in disbelief. Rose took her sleepwear seriously — pink, cute, and always matching.

Aster bit her lip. I guessed that was exactly what she had planned on wearing.

"I wonder what's keeping your father?" Mom said worriedly. "It's time for you girls to go home and get ready." She smiled. "And I really want you to come by the store so I can take your picture, Del! I can't wait to see you all dressed up for your very first formal dance!"

I looked around, slightly mortified. Luckily, the store was empty. Mom was making such a big deal out of this. But I couldn't argue, since I was picking up Amy and our store is on the way to her house.

"I'll be here," I told Mom.

Just then the phone rang, and Mom answered. "Petal

Pushers," she said. She listened for a moment. "Oh my poor baby. That's terrible. Oh, give her a big kiss for me. You stay there and take care of her. I'll figure something out. . . ." She hung up and looked at the three of us, her mouth set in a grim line.

"That was Daddy," she explained. "Girls, I have bad news. Poppy ate way too much candy at the birthday party. She has a terrible stomachache and Dad's afraid she's going to throw up!" She grimaced. "So he can't come in to help me with the last pickups tonight." She gave us a pleading look. "I hate to ask this, but could one of you stay here for a while?"

Fine with me!

"Sure!" I said to Mom. "No problem."

At the exact the same time, Aster practically jumped in the air and said, "I can do it!"

Rose stared at Aster, her mouth open. "This is the most important party of the school year," she said. "You *have* to go, Aster."

I gaped at Rose. I couldn't believe it — she was making the ultimate sacrifice. What a sister!

"So let Del stay," she concluded.

I snorted. I should have known.

136

"Actually, Mom, I don't mind staying at all," I spoke up. "I'll just call Amy and tell her I'll meet her at the dance later."

Aster leaned over and grabbed my arm. "No, Del," she said firmly. "I insist."

Rose shook her head emphatically. "No, Aster, if you're late you'll miss the makeovers! It's the best part!"

The word *makeovers* seemed to seal the deal for Aster. She took a deep breath and turned to her twin. "Rosie, I love you and I love that you want me to go to this party with you. But frankly, I would rather lick the bottom of the flower cooler than go to a girly-girl slumber party."

I stared at Aster. That was a lot of words in a row for her.

Rose's face fell. "But . . . I don't get it. You seemed so excited!"

Aster put an arm around her twin. "I was trying to be excited because *you* were so excited," she said.

"But it's the best party of the year," Rose said weakly.

"For you," said Aster. "I hate parties, Rose. You're going to have a great time. And you're going to have an even better time if you don't have to worry about me."

Mom dabbed her eyes with the day's bandanna, which happened to be purple. "My girls," she said. "You were both trying to make each other happy. That's really sweet." She blew her nose.

I grinned at Aster. "I thought you were going crazy! You agreed to do manicures and pedicures! You were going to wear a rhinestone T-shirt!"

Aster grinned back. "She's my twin," she said simply.

Rose smiled at Aster. "Thanks, sis," she said.

Mom ushered me and Rose out the door. "Hurry back!" she said.

And Aster waved to us merrily, a big grin on her face.

I brushed my hair until it was shining, parted it on the side, and pulled it back with a rhinestone barrette. My dress was pale blue with a matching bolero jacket and was actually supercute. I thought about Becky's pink dress that we'd bought together and my throat tightened. She still hadn't called me back. It was the longest we'd ever gone without speaking.

Pushing Becky out of my thoughts, I put on my white flats that were trimmed with blue rosettes. I swiped on some lip gloss of Mom's, then made a face at myself and swiped it right back off. Too sticky.

Rose met me at the bottom of the steps, in the pink

rhinestone T-shirt and a pair of capri jeans. Her Hello Kitty overnight bag was slung over her shoulder. What I wouldn't have given to see Aster in the very same outfit!

"Have a great time, girls," Dad said, giving us hugs. "And Del, as W. H. Auden once wrote, 'Dance till the stars come down from the rafters; Dance, dance, till you drop.'"

"Um . . . sure, Dad," I said.

He went back to tend to Poppy. He had set up the sick couch for her, which meant he had covered the couch with a sheet, added pillows and a soft, light green blanket, and placed the bathroom garbage can within easy reach. Poppy was watching *The Little Mermaid*, a glass of ginger ale on the coffee table in front of her.

"Bye, Poppy," Rose and I called. "Feel better!"

She stuck out her lower lip. "I'll never eat three Milky Ways in a row again!" she groaned.

"Followed by a pound of Twizzlers," said Dad, shaking his head.

Just thinking about all that sugar gave me a stomachache. Or maybe it was the thought of what was waiting for me at A Night in the Tropics. I wasn't quite sure.

❀　　❀　　❀

When we got to the store, a high school boy in his tux was just paying for his date's corsage. "Looks great," he called to Mom before he ran out the door. "Thanks!"

Mom clasped her hands together. "Oh, look at you both!" she squealed at me and Rose. "Let me take your picture!" She rushed off for her camera, then remembered my corsage. She disappeared into the cooler, and returned holding a box.

I opened the box. "Oh, Mom!" I breathed. It was a snap-on wrist corsage, the band covered in tiny, pale blue seed pearls. In the center was a cluster of creamy white roses and a sprig of Bells of Ireland, an elegant flower. The thinnest pale blue ribbons were looped between the blooms. It was stunning in its simplicity. And it would look amazing with my light blue dress.

"This must have taken you forever to make!" I said. "It's gorgeous!"

Ring-a-ling-ling. We looked up, expecting to see another out-of-breath high school student. But it was Great-aunt Lily.

She always looked well pulled together, but that night she looked extra fancy. She had on a cream-colored tweed suit with a pale green silk blouse underneath. She was wearing a hat I had never seen before, off-white with a sprig of pastel flowers. She was even wearing high heels!

"Looking good, Aunt Lily!" said Rose. Then she clapped her mouth shut, terrified that Aunt Lily was going to yell at her.

But Aunt Lily just looked pleased. Or maybe I should say, she didn't look totally annoyed, the way she usually did when confronted with the Bloom family. "I thought I would stop in on my way to the Library Gala," she said. "I heard you ended up doing quite a lively prom business!"

"We did," said Mom. "We really did."

"Congratulations!" said Aunt Lily. "I don't know how you managed to pull it off."

We all smiled. Another compliment from mean old Great-aunt Lily. Would wonders never cease?

Aunt Lily looked at the corsage box on the counter. "What a beautiful corsage," she said.

"Thank you," said Mom, blushing. She was unaccustomed to praise from her aunt. She looked almost confused.

"Is it for your dance, Del?" she asked me.

I stared at the corsage, then at Great-aunt Lily. Then I had an idea.

"No," I said. "It's for your gala!" I said, picking up the box and thrusting it into her hands.

"For me?" Aunt Lily said. She looked stunned for a moment. She picked it up, and was unsure of how to put it on. I snapped it on her wrist and she held it up in front of her face, admiring it.

"Thank you, Del," she said softly. "It's beautiful. I feel like a princess."

Rose smiled a big smile. Aster's eyes nearly popped out of her head.

"Congratulations on your prom business," said Aunt Lily. "And thank you for my wonderful corsage!"

We looked at one another in disbelief. Then she brought us all back down to earth, as only Aunt Lily can do.

"Just remember, you're going to need all the help you can get to keep the store afloat through the summer!"

We smiled at each other ruefully. *There* was the Aunt Lily we knew.

The door closed behind her. Mom shrugged. "Well, that was typical," she said, shaking her head. "But really, that was a lovely gesture, Del. Really lovely."

"Well, after that lame prom date of hers, it was about time she had a nice corsage!" I explained.

"Enough!" said Rose, grabbing my arm. "Can we please go?" she begged.

Aster waved good-bye and Mom gave us both kisses on our cheeks.

After I dropped Rose off at the party (the squeals were deafening!), I headed over to Amy's. I spotted the white stretch limo as soon as I turned the corner. Amber, her friends, and all their dates were posing in front of it. The boys looked handsome in their tuxes, and the girls' dresses were spectacular. It was like the high school version of the Academy Awards. One girl wore a floor-length, Grecian-style, one-shouldered dress, her hair in a cascade of golden curls. Another girl's hair was done up in hundreds of perfect tiny braids with sparkly crystal beads on them that exactly matched the icy blue of her silk, strapless gown. Another girl wore a short, glittery gold dress and matching strappy sandals that laced up her legs. But my favorite dress of all was Amber's: a simple black sheath, glammed up with a big pearl necklace.

I smiled. Each and every boy and girl was wearing a Petal Pushers signature corsage or boutonniere. Ponytail holders, rings, bracelets, purse corsages. Even one of Rose's ribbon chokers. I felt really proud of my family and all our hard work. This victory hadn't come easy. *Take that, Hamilton,* I thought.

The parents kept snapping pictures. "Over here!" and "Look at me!" they called, like a group of paparazzi.

"Enough, Mom," Amber groaned. "We're totally going to miss the prom!"

The kids started piling into the limo. As Amber was about to get in, she spotted me and gave me a wave. "You look great, Del!" she shouted.

I blushed a deep red as all her friends turned around to look at me. I waved at them awkwardly. "Have fun!" I called.

Amy finally came outside. She was wearing a 50s-style red halter dress with white polka dots. She looked very pretty. "Did you notice my shoes?" she said excitedly. They were white with red polka dots and had big red bows on them. They made her look a tiny bit like Minnie Mouse, but wisely, I kept that thought to myself. "Very cute!" I fibbed.

"You look very nice, too, Del," she said politely.

"Thanks," I replied. "Are you ready?"

It was time to find out what was going on with my best friend. Time to face seeing Hamilton and Ashley. Time to face the music.

Chapter Thirteen

Amy and I chatted as we walked, but the closer we got to school, the less we spoke. I think we were both nervous. I had no idea what I was going to do when I saw Becky. Especially when I saw her with a Fleur corsage on her wrist.

Outside the school, kids milled around the front entrance. Girls wearing shiny dresses in every color in Poppy's crayon box. Boys in jackets and ties, all with their hair combed neatly. Carmine was even wearing a tux. He looked nervous as he stood next to Penelope, who wore a white dress with spaghetti straps and a wide black sash.

"Hey, Carmine," I said as I got closer.

Looking panicked, he grabbed my arm. "Am I the only one in a tux?" he hissed. "Do I look like a waiter?"

"You look like James Bond," I assured him.

Carmine grinned. James Bond with curly black hair

and a slight overbite, to be completely truthful. But complete truths seemed unnecessary tonight.

Amy squeezed my hand. "We're going to have a great time," she said. "Even if we don't have dates!"

I squeezed right back.

I was surprised to see so many parents, posing their kids on the stairs as their flashes went off. I passed by Mike Hurley and his date on the steps. "No more pictures!" he whispered to his mom, who kept snapping away. "You're embarrassing me!"

I was grateful that Mom and Dad had let me come by myself. This prom was stressful enough without dealing with overeager parents!

Amy and I pushed through the crowd and got in line to hand over our tickets. I had a brief moment of panic as I fished through my mom's antique beaded purse. But then I spotted the ticket, which I had placed in the satiny pocket.

Mr. Rolando was behind the table, wearing a dark blue suit and a red tie.

"Good evening, Del, Amy," he boomed. "Welcome to A Night in the Tropics."

I smiled. It was funny to see him so dressed up, and

not in gym shorts and a polo shirt. Even stranger to see him without his whistle!

Amy stepped forward and I followed her through a clattering bamboo curtain and into the gymnasium. I blinked in surprise. I could hardly recognize the place. There were sparkling white lights and a disco ball hung from the ceiling. Multicolored balloons formed an arch over the refreshment table. This was no cold-pizza-and-flat-soda event. I could see real hors d'oeuvres on serving trays, and there was an actual drink station with a "bartender" serving up Shirley Temples and tropical drinks. One corner of the gym was filled with sand and tiki torches. It was stunningly tacky and also really, really fun.

I smiled as I saw some of my classmates balancing on a surfboard for their official middle school prom photo.

"Aloha, Del," said Ms. Studdert as she placed a brightly colored plastic lei around my neck.

"Aloha, Ms. Studdert," I said, getting into the spirit of things.

I spotted Ashley, in an off-white strapless dress that fell nearly to the floor and an expensive looking tiara in her hair, holding court and greeting students as if she was the hostess. I steered clear of that side of the room.

Kids were standing around in groups, talking and laughing nervously. I felt a small tremor of excitement as I stood on my tiptoes, scanning the crowd. I spotted Amy's rejected date, Jimmy, heading our way with Eleni.

I turned to Amy. "Jimmy's coming over," I warned. "Promise me you're not going to get upset."

She nodded. "No problem. I'm totally over it." Then her eyes widened. "Now promise me that you won't . . ."

I looked up. I was face-to-face with Bob. Shockingly enough, he appeared to have a date.

"Hey, Delfoodcoloring," said Bob.

I grimaced at him. Then I turned to his date. "Uh, hi, Cici," I said. I stared at her, wondering why in the world she agreed to go to the dance with Sarah Josepha Hale's biggest bully. To each her own, I guess.

"Dateless, I see?" he said charmingly.

"I'm here with friends," I snapped, indicating Amy. "Heard of the concept?"

Bob scowled. Oops, had I hit on a sore point? I was surprised to find that I felt a little bad. So I smiled at him and Cici. "Have fun tonight," I said.

"Thanks, Del," said Cici. Bob just looked surprised.

I rejoined Amy. "That wasn't so terrible," I said. "How about you?"

She sighed. "I felt a little awkward seeing the two of them together," she admitted. "But not as awkward as I'll feel when I see Brian. I wonder if he brought a date?"

"I guess we'll find out soon enough," I said.

Just then a Beyoncé song came on and all the girls squealed and rushed the dance floor. Amy grabbed my hand and pulled me along. On the way I spotted Heather. She was sitting on a folding chair, looking bored. Behind her, I saw Billy and his soccer buddies, pushing and shoving each other and acting like, well, boys at a school dance.

"I'll meet you on the dance floor in a minute," I said to Amy.

"I'm going to look like a loser, dancing by myself!" she complained. "Oh, look, there's Jessica and Jackson!" She danced over to them.

I made my way past my dancing classmates to Heather. I sat on the cold metal chair next to her.

"Having fun hanging out with the soccer team?" I couldn't resist asking.

She sighed. "You were right, Del," she said. "And so was

Jessica. I can't believe I thought I'd have a good time at the dance with Billy. Popular does not equal fun," she added sadly. "The only thing we have in common is that we both think he's cute."

I couldn't help but giggle at this.

"Surprisingly enough, I think Becky was right, too," Heather added.

"Becky?" I said. Hearing her name made my blood run cold. "Have you seen her? What do you mean?"

Heather smiled. "I'll let her tell you herself." She stood up. "I think she's by the refreshment table. Meanwhile, I'm going to go dance with Amy and Jessica." She glanced back at the horseplaying boys. "I doubt my date will even notice." She laughed ruefully and headed off.

I took a deep breath. So Becky was here. I wasn't sure what I would say to her or even if I wanted to give her a chance to explain herself. I didn't get to think about it for long. The next thing I knew, Becky had plopped down on the chair next to me.

"Del," she said rather coldly.

"Becky," I responded tersely.

"That was some message you left me," she said.

I sucked in my cheeks and stared at my white flats. "What do you expect when you shop at the competition?" I demanded, not meeting her eye. "You know how important Petal Pushers is to me. And you completely betrayed me by going to Fleur."

Becky's icy composure broke. "I know," she said, her voice shaky. I looked at her, and she was holding back tears. "I felt terrible about it. But I didn't have a choice."

All of a sudden it all made perfect, horrible sense. My mouth fell open and I felt a huge lump in my throat. I couldn't even look at her.

"You went to Fleur because you have a crush on Hamilton," I said flatly.

Becky laughed. "What? Are you crazy? Oh, Del, don't be ridiculous."

A terrific sense of relief washed over me. "So then why did you go get your corsage at Fleur when I offered you a free one from Petal Pushers?" I didn't even give her a chance to answer. "I can only imagine what it looks like," I said snottily, grabbing her wrist to take a look.

And I gasped. Around Becky's slim wrist was the beautiful corsage that Mom had made. The one with the butterfly delicately perched on the pink and purple hydrangeas. The one commissioned by the nice boy to give to the smartest and prettiest girl in the whole school.

I stared at Becky, totally confused. "But . . ."

"My corsage *is* from Petal Pushers," Becky said simply. "My date bought it for me there." She lowered her gaze and stared at her delicate silver shoes. "I was embarrassed to tell you I had a date," she explained. "I mean, when Amy and Jessica and Heather were talking about dates, you always acted like you thought that stuff was ridiculous, and that you expected me to side with you on it."

I felt a stab of guilt. I *had* always assumed Becky and I were on the same page with everything. It had never occurred to me that we might feel differently about certain things. And, I realized, I *did* kind of care about boys and dates and stuff like that. Why else had I gotten so upset about Ashley and Hamilton?

"I'm sorry about that," I said. "I wish you felt like you could tell me!"

"I tried a few times," Becky said, shrugging. "But you didn't make it easy . . ."

"So who *is* your date?" I asked.

She took a big breath. "It's Matt," she said softly.

"Matt!" I cried. "You mean Bob's friend? No! It can't be. He's such a . . ."

Becky shook her head, smiling. "Actually, Del, he's great. We started talking in the library one day after school and he's really interesting. And funny! He knows that Bob can be an idiot, but he feels bad for him because he doesn't have that many friends. He was glad when your teacher gave him a new lab partner. He says he's been getting good grades on his labs for the first time all year!"

"But . . ."

Becky looked at me. "Del, I never have crushes on boys. Never. He's just so nice. And he's totally into astronomy, just like me." She looked into my eyes. "You're my best friend. Would I agree to go to the dance with someone who wasn't . . ." Then she said a word I never expected to hear come out of her mouth. "Crushworthy?"

I gave her a small apologetic grin. "I believe you," I said. Then I told her the story Mom had told me about the corsage.

Becky looked pleased, but totally embarrassed. "So now you get it?"

"Now I get it," I said. "But one thing still doesn't make sense. Why *were* you at Fleur?"

Becky looked away. "Well, I had to buy Matt a boutonniere. Since I hadn't told you I had a date I couldn't exactly buy it from Petal Pushers, could I?"

"I guess not," I admitted. I took a deep breath. "I'm so sorry for making you sneak around like that."

Becky looked at me, her face serious. "Del, you made it really hard for me to tell you about Matt. You hated him just because he was friends with Bob. You never gave him a chance."

"Oh, Becky," I said. "Here it was, your first date and you had to hide it from me. I want you to know that from now on you can always tell me everything."

"I will. I promise," said Becky.

We stood and I gave her a hug. "Big Fat Friendship?" I said.

Becky laughed. "Big Fat Friendship," she replied. We had started that back in first grade. We were both totally convinced that's what BFF stood for until one of our classmates corrected us. But we liked it better that way and it stuck.

Another good song started playing. "Go dance with Matt," I said. "I'll find you guys later."

"Thanks, Del," said Becky as she disappeared into the crowd.

Feeling a little bit shaken, I wandered over to the refreshment table. I realized I was thirsty. I went up to the bartender and ordered something from the drink menu called a Coconut Dream. He served up its frosty deliciousness in an actual coconut cup that came with a bendy straw. The student council had really gone all out.

"Fancy!" I said.

I grabbed a couple of pigs in a blanket (my favorite hors d'oeuvres ever) and some mustard. I had just crammed a pig into my mouth when someone approached me.

It was Hamilton Baldwin, super spy.

Now I just want to make this clear: His spying and my two spying attempts needed to be held under two different microscopes. I had spied to confirm bad behavior on Fleur's part. He had spied to gather secret information from me and my family. He was a bad spy and I was a good spy. End of story.

"I'm glad to see you're okay," he said. He was looking very serious and concerned.

I gulped. If I thought he'd looked cute in his yellow-

and-purple gym clothes, I was not prepared for Hamilton in his middle school prom best. Dark gray, pin-striped suit. Light blue shirt. Purple-and-blue tie. I looked down. Shiny black oxfords. He caught me checking out his shoes and playfully lifted up his pant leg. "Light blue socks, too," he said with a grin.

But I was not about to be charmed by his ability to match.

"Hey," I said coolly.

"So, are you okay?" he asked.

"Sure," I replied. "Why wouldn't I be okay?"

"I saw what happened," he said, his eyes sympathetic.

"You did?" I said. I didn't realize that he knew Becky and I weren't getting along. Not, I reminded myself, that it was any of his business.

"I can't believe Bob brought Cici!" He shook his head. "What a jerk!"

Huh? I stared at Hamilton, trying to figure out what was going on. "It *is* surprising that he actually got a member of the opposite sex to go out with him," I agreed. "But that's not the reason he's a jerk!"

Hamilton smiled at me gently like I was a small, confused

child. "Del, your date showed up with someone else. You don't have to act tough around me. It's got to hurt."

I had just taken a big swig of my drink and nearly spit Coco Lopez and pineapple juice all over Hamilton's blue shirt and skinny tie.

"My date!" I managed to say. "Bob is not my date!"

"That's right, he's Cici's date," Hamilton explained to me patiently. "But he was supposed to be here with you."

I looked right into his eyes. "I have no idea what you are talking about," I said. "I would never go on a date with Bob Zimmer!"

Hamilton looked totally bewildered. He ran his hand through his sandy hair. "Well, that's what Ashley told me after gym class," he said. "And then I went to the flower store where you work, and you confirmed it. You told me that that he was assigned to be your date. Remember?"

I started laughing. I laughed long and hard. Then I set down my coconut cup and wiped the tears from my eyes. "I meant that Bob had been assigned to be my *lab partner*," I said. "Have you ever heard of a teacher assigning you a date?" I put my hand to my head. "Jeez, what kind of school did you go to before this one?"

Hamilton looked totally sheepish. "I *did* think that sounded really weird," he said.

A lightbulb went off. "But — but — but — I thought you came to the store to steal my family's prom flower ideas. So you weren't spying?"

"Spying?" said Hamilton, frowning. "What am I, one of the Hardy Boys? Spying on what? I just wanted to talk to you. I kept missing you at school." Then he paused. "Wait . . . what did you say about your family?"

"So you really don't know?" I asked.

"Don't know what?"

I took a deep breath. "We're rivals," I finally said.

"Rivals?"

"Petal Pushers, the store you came to visit me at, is owned by my family."

Hamilton looked surprised. Very surprised. "I didn't know that," he said.

I believed him.

He grinned. "I guess that explains your name," he said.

I nodded. "And I know that your mom owns Fleur," I added.

"How do you know?" he asked curiously.

Oh, I shouldn't have said that, I thought. How was I going to explain that one? I decided to go with complete disclosure. "Well, um, when Fleur first opened, I went to check it out and I met the owner. Then when I saw you with her at the video store I realized she was your mother."

Hamilton nodded. "So you spied on Fleur," he said, trying to keep a straight face.

"I'd prefer to call it a friendly visit," I said, my cheeks getting hot. This next part was going to be hard, but I felt like I had to come totally clean. "Then, when I thought that you had spied on our ideas, I went to your mom's store to check."

"So you're constantly casing the joint, I see," he said with a smirk.

I gave him a dirty look and soldiered on.

"And I heard your mom say that she had an idea to get the high school kids into the store, so I assumed you had told her secret information."

Hamilton laughed and laughed. "Wait till you hear what her brilliant idea was. Prom hats!" he said. "Straw hats with flowers attached. They didn't exactly fly off the shelves."

I grimaced, wondering if my disguise had been the inspiration. Well, that was final confirmation that no spying had occurred. On his part, anyway. As for myself, it was definitely time to hang up my magnifying glass.

He shook his head. "That's pretty funny," he said. "Rival florists — ooh."

"It's not funny at all," I bristled. "It's weird. And awkward."

"Weird how?"

"Because we're in competition with each other," I explained. "We both want the same business. Like we were just both competing for the prom."

Hamilton shrugged. "I don't know why you think it's such a big deal. I don't have anything to do with the store," he said. "My stepfather bought it for my mom when we moved here. I mean, sure, sometimes I hear them talking about flowers at the dinner table." He grinned. "Weren't you impressed when I knew what a delphinium was?"

"I certainly was," I said.

"But I'm a boy, Del. Flowers are just not my thing."

Whew. I hadn't considered that before. I thought about the situation for a moment. "Well, how about if from now on we never discuss business with each other?"

"No problem there," said Hamilton.

"And we stay away from each other's stores. Just to be safe."

"Agreed," said Hamilton.

There was one more thing. I narrowed my eyes at him. "So where's your date?"

"My date?" he said. "Enlighten me. Who's supposed to be my date?"

"I heard you were going with . . . Ashley," I said, looking at the ground.

"Ashley?" he said. "What makes you think I asked Ashley? I didn't ask anyone." He looked at me and took a deep breath. "Actually," he began. "Actually . . ."

"Yes?" I said.

"Actually there is someone I wanted to ask . . ."

I gulped. "Oh yeah?" I said warily.

Just then Jessica and Jackson and Amy came running over. Mr. Rolando had gone into the gym supply closet and taken out a high jump bar. He held one side and

Ms. Studdert held the other. The DJ put on some calypso music. And we all lined up to do the limbo.

"How low can you go?" Mr. Rolando started the chant.

The bar started out pretty high, and we all made it underneath. As the bar got lower and lower kids started dropping out. I was on line in front of Hamilton. As I began to inch forward, Hamilton grabbed my hand and we limboed together. We high-fived when we emerged on the other side — we'd made it!

I can't believe it, I thought to myself. *Hamilton held my hand!*

Ashley stood to the side, looking disgruntled. I wasn't sure if it was because she couldn't limbo in her expensive designer dress. Or maybe it was because Hamilton and I were having such a fun time together. Possibly both.

But I didn't give her another thought.

As a new song started, I looked around at my friends, all dancing and laughing. Becky and I were best friends again. Hamilton and Ashley hadn't gone to the prom together. And Petal Pushers was going to be okay.

There was just one problem. Hamilton never finished his sentence. And I was too embarrassed to ask him to.

Chapter Fourteen

The next morning, my feet ached. We had danced and laughed and eaten way too many pigs in a blanket. I had taken several pictures on the surfboard: one with all my friends, one with Becky, and one with Hamilton as Ashley glared from across the room.

I had to admit it. Despite my reservations and all of the drama, A Night in the Tropics had been a pretty cool idea. I even told Ashley so on the way out. She stood there, her mouth open like a gasping fish, unsure how to react to a compliment from me. I'm sure she thought I was being sarcastic. But I wasn't, not at all. It had been one of the most fun nights of my life.

I hadn't even eaten my breakfast yet and I had already been on the phone with each of my friends. Twice with

Becky. Dad had to call me three times before I finally made my way downstairs to the breakfast table.

"Del, I can't wait for . . ." Poppy said.

"Shhhh!" I told her.

Mom looked at us curiously. "What's going on, girls?" she asked.

I gave Aster a curious look. Was it time to fill them in? My sister nodded.

"Just be prepared to have some fun tonight," I told them. "We're foregoing our Sunday Movie Night for something completely different."

Dad put down the Arts section and leaned forward. "Sounds intriguing!" he said.

"Living room at six o'clock," I said. "Be there. Wear your eighties best."

"Our eighties best?" Dad echoed. "You mean outfits from the olden days?"

I nodded, grinning.

Mom laughed. "No fair! You have to tell us what's going on!" she said. "I can't wait till six o'clock!"

"It's a . . ." Poppy started to say.

Aster put her hand over Poppy's mouth.

". . . surprise," I finished. "It's a surprise. You'll just have to wait."

Rose returned home that afternoon, looking exhausted.

"How was it?" Mom wanted to know.

"Amazing," she said. "We did makeovers, and talked about boys, and played Truth or Dare, and gave each other manicures." She smiled. "It was so cool." She turned to her twin. "And you were so right. You would have hated every minute of it! I'm so glad you weren't there!"

Aster smiled. "I am, too!" she said sweetly.

I swear, I'll never figure out my sisters.

Finally, it was time for my sisters and me to put our surprise plan into action. We sent Mom and Dad upstairs, with strict instructions not to come back down until we were ready for them.

Then we moved furniture, decorated the living room, and argued over the order of our playlist. Finally, I gave Poppy the thumbs-up.

"Ready!" Poppy called up the stairs excitedly.

Their bedroom door squeaked open and Mom and Dad walked down the stairs. For the very first time, I was glad that my parents never throw away anything. Mom was wearing black leggings, and a lime-green shirt with a bright pink paisley print and huge shoulder pads. She had black rubber bracelets up and down both arms. Dad had on a very large blazer, a skinny leather tie, and these weird shoes that he said were called Capezios. They both had moussed their hair as large as humanly possible. I stifled a guffaw. They looked positively ridiculous. And these weren't costumes. My parents had actually worn these clothes twenty-five years ago. In public.

They both glanced around the living room, looking confused. The lights were low, the rug was rolled up, and the furniture was pushed into the corners. We had taken down one of Mom's hanging plants and replaced it with the disco ball I had convinced Mr. Rolando to let me borrow after the dance last night. I had somehow managed to smuggle it home under my bolero jacket without anyone noticing.

"Ready?" asked Rose.

"Ready!" I said.

Aster hit PLAY on the iPod and "Forever Young" by Alphaville came on, the first song in the greatest hits of the '80s playlist she had put together over the past week.

"This was my prom song!" cried Mom.

"Welcome to the prom you never had!" I told them.

Their eyes brightened as they realized what we had done. Then Mom and Dad grinned and immediately began to slow dance together. Rose handed Mom a pink bandanna so she could wipe the happy tears that were streaming down her face.

We clapped as the song ended. And Dad spun Mom around in a little circle.

"This is so much fun!" said Dad. "I feel like a teenager."

"Well, just wait for the next song," said Aster with a grin.

It was an old song called "Rock Lobster" — my dad said it was by a band called the B-52s. My parents immediately started bouncing up and down.

I looked at my sisters, my eyebrows raised. What was *that* all about?

"Believe it or not, this is the way we danced in the eighties!" said Mom. "Come, girls, join us!"

Poppy squealed with delight as she started jumping up and down in place. Rose was next. Aster and I shrugged at each other and joined in.

My phone started vibrating. I had a text message. I stopped dancing for a moment, pulled it out of my pocket, and read the message. It was from an unfamiliar number, and it read:

WHEN I SAID I WANTED 2 ASK SOMEONE 2 PROM — IT WAS U. HB.

HB. Hamilton Baldwin. So Heather was right. He *did* like me. My heart stood still for a brief second. Then a big grin spread across my face. I was ready to admit it. I had a big bad crush on Hamilton Baldwin. And it appeared he felt the same way.

"It wasn't a rock. It was a rock lobster!" the song blared happily.

I snapped the phone shut and placed it back in my pocket. I grabbed Poppy's hands and her face lit up as we started jumping up and down together. I was definitely bouncing higher than before.

I looked around at my crazy family. We had done it again, by the skin of our teeth. But Aunt Lily was probably right. There would be another crisis next week, another client to fight for. We wouldn't be able to rest for a moment.

But if anyone could pull it off, it was us.

Turn the page for a sneak peek at the next Petal Pushers book!

I hate having a summer birthday. I've never had cupcakes in the classroom, the whole class singing "Happy Birthday" to me. Just once I'd like to have my friends around to help me celebrate. But they're always on vacation. And for some reason, this year seemed worse than usual. I guess it was because I was about to turn thirteen. You know, the first birthday as a teenager and all that. You were supposed to do something special. Jessica, always up for something different, had taken us to our very first roller derby match. Amy had turned thirteen in March and had had a big bat mitzvah at the Country Club, complete with a DJ and karaoke machine. Heather and Becky wouldn't turn thirteen till October and November, respectively. But they both had big plans.

And then there was me. Birth date: July 7. Birthstone: ruby. Sign: Cancer. Flower: larkspur. Best birthday gift: my dog, Buster, when I was six. Best birthday party: none. No doubt about it, summer birthdays bite.

I turned around to head outside and meet up with my friends when I spotted Carmine Belloni across the hallway. He was leaning against his locker and studying a rectangular piece of paper.

Carmine looked up. "Hey, Del," he said. "Are you going to the party, too? It's at that new catering place that's supposed to be really cool."

"What party?" I asked, interested. Was someone having an end-of-year party? That would be fun! It would take my mind off being abandoned by all my friends for the summer, at least for a while.

Carmine held up the paper he had been looking at. It was a fancy invitation, thick and cream colored. Gilt letters spelled out *Ashley's Thirteenth Birthday*.

Ohhhhhh, I thought, instantly understanding why I hadn't received one. "Ashley and I aren't exactly best buds," I explained to him.

"Oh, sorry, Del," he said.

"No problem," I said with a shrug. But I couldn't take my eyes off the invite. And I gasped when I saw the date — July seventh. I couldn't even get four friends together, and Ashley Edwards was going to have a huge party! Not on her actual birthday, which is in mid-July, may I add.

On *mine*.

Cinderella CLEANERS

ONE GIRL. LOTS OF CLOTHES.
ENDLESS OPPORTUNITIES FOR ADVENTURE . . .

Change of a Dress

Prep Cool

Rock & Role

Mask Appeal

Scheme Spirit

Swan Fake